Amani was waiting for the distant clock to clang its single note which would echo over the city. That was when he would break into a run, screaming abuse before he littered the street with dead and dying innocents. His only regret was that he would not be able to view the mangled corpses and hear the screams of the wounded.

Satanic Armageddon

A Black Fedora Story

Guy N. Smith

Other books by Guy N. Smith:

WEREWOLF OMNIBUS
THE CHARNEL CAVES: A CRABS NOVEL
SABAT 6: THE RETURN
TALES FROM THE GRAVEYARD
THE CASEBOOK OF RAYMOND ODELL

Further books by the Sinister Horror Company:

WHAT GOOD GIRLS DO – *Jonathan Butcher*

MARKED – *Stuart Park*

FOREST UNDERGROUND – *Lydian Faust*

CANNIBAL NUNS FROM OUTER SPACE! – *Duncan P. Bradshaw*

PUNCH – *J. R. Park*
DEATH DREAMS IN A WHOREHOUSE – *J. R. Park*
MAD DOG – *J. R. Park*

BREAKING POINT – *Kit Power*

HELL SHIP – *Benedict J. Jones*

MANIAC GODS – *Rich Hawkins*

Visit SinisterHorrorCompany.com for further information on these and other titles.

PRESENTS

THE MASTER OF PULP HORROR

GUY N. SMITH

Satanic Armageddon: A Black Fedora Story

Edited by J. R. Park
Design by J. R. Park
Cover art by Mike McGee

Published by The Sinister Horror Company

Satanic Armageddon -- 1st ed.
ISBN 978-1-912578-31-3

THE SINISTER CHAMPIONS

Anthony Watson, Chris Hall,
David Lars Chamberlain, Emma Audsley,
Gary Harper, James Steel, Jason Kelly,
Jorge Wiles, Matt Shaw, Paul M. Feeney,
Rebekah Mann, Steve Matthewman,
Thomas Joyce, Tracy Fahey
& Wayne Parkin

Thank you for your support.

To become a Sinister Champion, visit our Patreon page for details at:

www.patreon.com/SinisterHorrorCompany

Other adventures of John Mayo, the man in the black fedora, can be found in:

The Black Fedora,
first published in 1991

The Knighton Vampires,
first published in 1993

The Grim Reaper: A Black Fedora Story,
first published in 1997

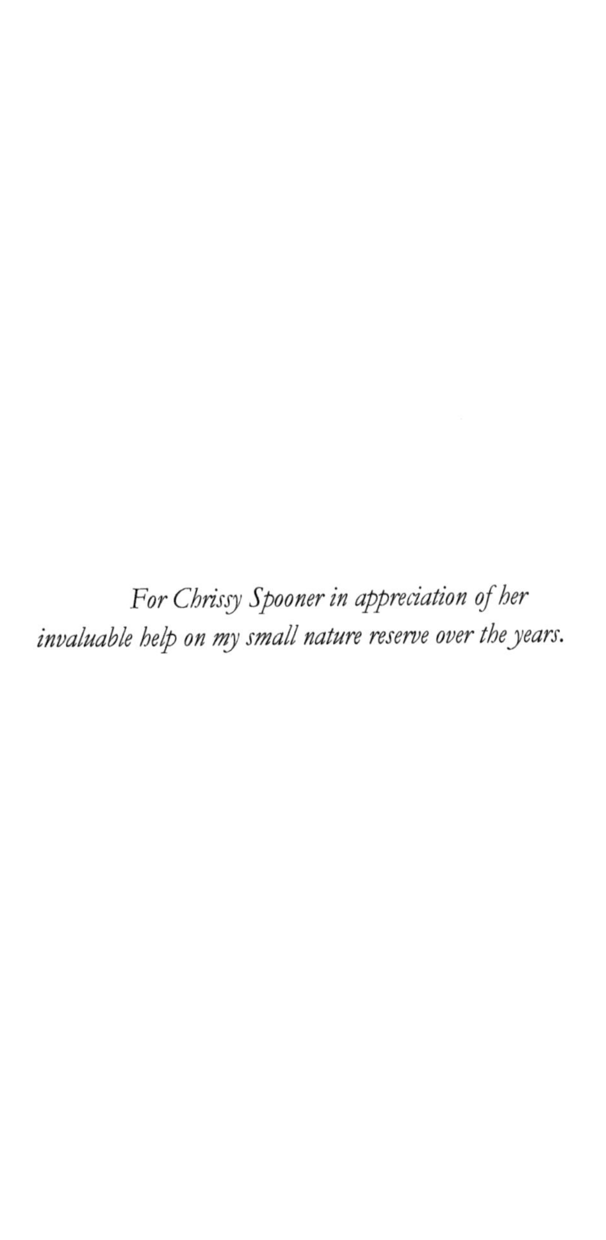

For Chrissy Spooner in appreciation of her invaluable help on my small nature reserve over the years.

My Introduction to the Black Fedora at a Church Wedding

I never cease to be amazed at the strange places in which ideas for books and characters crop up. Possibly the strangest of all occasions occurred at the wedding of two friends.

As we all filed into the church, I noted with some surprise a young man wearing a broad brimmed black hat which he made no effort to remove. As he seated himself in a pew the vicar came down from the pulpit and asked him to remove his headgear!

I was intrigued and after the service I made a point of approaching this somewhat strange guest. His name was Martin and he was exceedingly flattered when I told him that I was an author and that his hat had just given me an idea for a character in a forthcoming novel.

'It's called a fedora,' he told me. 'I picked it up in a second-hand clothing store. Tell you what,

I'll lend it to you. Look after it and I'll give you a call at a later date and maybe fetch it back.'

So that was how it was left on that memorable day. I had the fedora and my next task was to create a character and a plot for the book.

In the week's that followed everything came together. An unusual hat demanded an unusual character to wear it, along with dark clothing. All very sinister. Thus, John Mayo was born, a somewhat sinister individual, a loner who worked for Operation Werewolf, allied to Scotland yard's anti-terrorist force. It was during this period that his wife died suddenly, a devastating blow to Mayo. The department had given him leave and during that time he travelled to Knighton in Wales where he finds himself involved in a sinister encounter with "vampires". In due course he returned to his employers. Eventually he "retired" but was still "on call" if something arose which baffled the team of investigators. In 2006 his former employers became known as Counter Terrorism Command but nothing else changed.

Mayo was enjoying a peaceful retirement when he was summoned to investigate a terrifying case which threatened the democracy of both the UK and Europe. He had encountered the vampire threat in the past but now he was up against an enemy which was under the control of satanic forces.

It was the greatest and most deadly challenge of his long career.

I still had that fedora of Martin's on loan. About a year after acquiring it I was invited to take part in a "horror evening" at Llandovery in Wales. Here I was requested to go on the small stage and give a short talk to the audience. At the conclusion of this Martin appeared, pre-planned, to demand the return of his now famous headgear. Shrugging my shoulders, I reluctantly handed it over.

Then somebody in the audience stood up and an identical hat came spinning onto the stage "you can keep that" the benefactor shouted amidst cheers. Clearly my fans were determined that I was not to lose a fedora which had spawned two best-selling novels set in their home territory!

Guy N. Smith

Chapter One

'Great to see you again, Mayo,' the tall, slightly stooped man rose from behind his desk, extending a welcoming hand. 'Good god, twenty-five years or so since we last saw each other, that time when you bought that gang of pseudo vampires to book in Wales. Seems like only yesterday and I'm retiring at the end of next year.'

His visitor nodded, merely grunted a reply as he lowered himself into the proffered chair opposite. John Mayo was of indeterminable age though he had to be in his early sixties with pale blue eyes and pallid features made all the more so by the jet black broad brimmed fedora which possibly hid greying hair. He rarely removed his headgear; it was an integral part of one who had worn it for it most of his life. His dark matching bomber jacket and corduroy trousers added to a somewhat sinister appearance. In many ways Detective Inspector Charlie Wells was encouraged by this. It was somewhat reassuring to note that the other had changed little if any, over the years.

'You took some finding, Mayo.' A rare half smile. 'In fact, I almost believed that you had retired. I had nearly given up until I chanced to meet Ernie Watts, a former employee of this unit and, somewhat reluctantly, he gave me your address, your hidey-hole, so to speak. Anyway, I've found you and you've been good enough to agree to a meeting. Are you still working for want of a better description of your somewhat mysterious lifestyle?'

'It all depends,' the other was somewhat hesitant in his reply. 'If I fancy a mission, I take it but it has to inspire me. I'm not a Private Eye in the accepted sense of the word. I've done maybe half a dozen investigations since that business in Knighton, no more. Anyway, curiosity prompted me to answer your call, I'm not promising anything, but I guess it wouldn't be any run-of-the-mill problem you've got. So fire away.'

'As you are aware, Mayo,' Wells settled himself back in his chair, 'we are a special offshoot of MI5. We merged some time ago with the anti-terrorism branch of the Metropolitan Police. This department was formed in 2006 and is known as Counter Terrorism Command. We operate independently and the public are not aware of our existence. Our officers arrest suspected spies as MI5 are not authorised to effect this. Between ourselves we have removed some highly dangerous ISIS members in recent years. Now we are faced with the biggest and most dangerous challenge of all.'

'Go on,' Mayo leaned forward, his lips pursed. Clearly he had not been summoned to investigate a run-of-the-mill episode. He was intrigued.

'As you are doubtless aware,' the other continued, 'knife and gun crime in the UK is at an all-time high. For instance, only last week there were four street stabbings in Birmingham in five days. This was followed by two random shootings in Manchester.'

'Drug gang warfare,' Mayo interrupted.

'Yes, but there's more to it than just that. These apparently random crimes are organised by the most dangerous master criminal of all time, not just in the UK but across Europe. We have managed to intercept some bomb plots but they are only a few of what is building up into a massive destruction of human life. Reduced police on the streets cannot cope with 'stop and search'. Our agents have discovered that this destruction is organised by Leonid Zinovsky, the most wanted terrorist in Eastern Europe, who works with virtually every organisation, causing mayhem and loss of life. Mass killings in Paris, Belgium the Middle East you name it and he is behind it. His followers are known as 'The Moon People'.'

'So, where do I figure in this?'

'I guess you're the man for the job, Mayo. We've already lost one of our agents so I want you to be aware of what you're taking on. That is, if you are agreeable to working for the department.'

'Fill me in on the details.'

'As you know a number of youngsters are being radicalised. Zinovsky is recruiting drug addicts, running a massive drug trade in which those concerned fall into his powers. Teenagers vanish from respectable homes, go abroad to join

ISIS and other factions. Mostly they disappear, victims of warfare or murdered. A few weeks ago, we were contacted about one Gemma Jones, a Welsh teenager who just walked out on her parents. They're frantic. Anyway, one of our agents, Bill Williamson, tracked her to a deserted farmhouse in the Welsh Hills which was being used by Zinovsky as a HQ, albeit temporary. That was the last we heard of Bill, he just vanished, probably murdered and his corpse disposed of. Anyway, it would appear from his last report that this farmhouse is a temporary 'temple' for want of a better description. We've checked it out, there are signs of occult activity having taken place there, a meeting place for radicalisation etc. Nevertheless, it's a starting place for an investigation and I believe you are the man for this. Well, what do you think?'

'I'll give it a go,' Mayo's answer was instant. 'I'll go and take a look around in broad daylight, check that it's empty, see if there are any clues to what is going on there. Depending on what I find, if anything, I'll play it from there.'

'Good,' there was no mistaking the relief in the other's voice. 'I must make it clear, though, that you're on your own. Fill me in on anything you find but we avoid publicity. If, like Williamson, you disappear then we can't publicise it. You have a double mission, find Gemma Jones and get her out of wherever she is before she disappears abroad. If you can find out what has happened to Williamson it will go on the records but no further.'

'What about Zinovsky and the occult connection?'

'I take the occult factor with a pinch of salt. Personally, I believe it's a mode of fear instilled into Zinovsky's followers, all part of radicalisation, but I keep on open mind. We believe that he is currently in the UK although he could vanish overseas at any time. If you can find him then that's a real bonus.'

'And if I do?'

'Kill him! Leave his body where it can be found. That will be a big blow to his organisation. Doubtless he has intimate followers. Kill them, too, if you get the chance. This whole business is building up to a massive takeover of the UK by crazed radicalists who will stop at nothing. The plot is to have the UK and the rest of the world under their rule. Civilizations will be bombed or shot. Time is running out. Get yourself picked up by them, infiltrate their ranks. I can't advise you any further. Destroy them if the opportunity arises. I'll leave it up to you, Mayo. You're on your own. There are no rules to play by.'

'I'll do what I can,' John Mayo stood up adjusting his fedora. 'I'll be in touch... maybe. Wish me luck.'

'Before you go,' Wells produced a couple of photographs from the drawer of his desk, 'take a look at these. The missing girl, Gemma Jones, and our agent Williamson, just so you will recognise them if you come across them.'

Mayo studied the printout, nodded.

'Oh, just one more thing. It is believed, not yet proved, that bin Laden's son, Hamza bin Laden, is emerging as the leader of Al-Qaeda, seeking to avenge his father's killing. Like Zinovsky, he's something of a shadow. Currently the Americans have put up a one million-dollar bounty for his capture. I just thought it worth mentioning.'

'I read it in the papers,' Mayo smiled. 'I'll add him to my list just in case I come across him. You've given me plenty to go on. I'll keep you posted.'

Wells sat staring at the wall long after his visitor had left. A final effort on his part to combat the evil which was fast taking over the UK. There could be no better agent than the man in the black fedora, of that he was convinced. A niggling thought troubled his conscience that he had condemned Mayo to an unspeakable death if the other fell into the hands of Zinovsky and his followers. He brushed it aside. Several of the department agents had lost their lives doing jobs in which they knew the risks. His own job was to deploy them into unspeakable danger. Maybe he had just sent Mayo to his death. He shook his head, his thoughts turned to his forthcoming retirement. Maybe then he could relax with a clear conscience.

Chapter Two

'I thought you had retired!' There was a note of shock bordering on anger in the attractive woman's tone. Gwenda had been Mayo's live-in partner for the past decade. Marriage had been mentioned on numerous occasions, but it had never materialised. They were happy enough in their Gloucestershire cottage and saw no reason to change their status.

She was petite with short fair hair which successfully hid any signs of grey. Thirty years younger than her partner, age was not a problem. Mayo was active, satisfied her in every way. She prayed that it might be so for many years yet.

There had been few calls upon his ability to investigate any unusual cases beyond the powers and capabilities of the police in recent years. She had prayed that there would not be any more. But now...

'Well, what is it this time?' she snapped, hands on hips, her pale blue eyes meeting those of her partners. 'Can't this special force, whatever they call themselves, sort out their own problems without calling you in to help them?'

'Apparently not on this occasion,' his voice was soft, he shook his head. 'I can't go into details, I'm sworn to secrecy but hopefully I won't be away for too long, a week or two at the most. And if I don't find what I'm looking for then I'll pack it in. I'll just say that a teenage girl has vanished from her home, her folks are frantic and I'm determined to find her before she comes to any serious harm.'

Gwenda's expression softened. 'Well, in that case I can't argue. But these days young girls are getting kidnapped, raped and murdered on almost a daily basis. I just hope you find her alive and unharmed, John.'

'I will do my best,' he turned away and went through to the adjoining room where his .38 handgun had lain hidden in a drawer for several years.

Mayo left home in the early afternoon, embarked upon the long drive up to Mid Wales. He needed to arrive in time to find secure parking for his Mini Clubman 4x4 and book in at a B&B. Presteigne was as good a place as any to begin his quest, numerous youth had moved in here, living on social security and there was a growing drug problem. Recently there had been some incidents of violence on the streets late at night.

A youth pressed against a door, half hidden, stepped out in front of him, his features masked by shadow.

'Only a fiver,' he had a plastic packet in his hand.

Mayo slowed his steps, his hand dropped into his pocket. The feel of that handgun was somewhat reassuring.

'I'm skint till I get my social security tomorrow. Maybe we could meet up someplace then, do a deal.'

'Fuck off!' An angry hiss.

Mayo's instinct told him that this was a lone pusher, just out to make a few quid, nothing to do with the Moon People. He walked on, increasing his pace.

'Hi, there!' A female voice came from a darkened passageway adjoining a couple of premises. He halted, peered, made out a slim girl pressed up against the wall.

There was a tense silence, each sizing up the other.

'Can't we find somewhere more comfortable than a stand-up job in a draughty passage?

He moved out into the light cast by a nearby streetlamp and he saw a slim, petite figure wearing a sweater and jeans, long fair hair falling about her shoulders.

'Maybe,' she smiled, 'but how do I know that you're not a cop?'

'Because if I was, I would have arrested you here and now for soliciting on the street.'

'Sure, there's a better place but it's not around town. We have to meet up another night, I'd arrange for a friend to take us because it's a mile or two out-of-town.'

'I see. A brothel?'

'Sort of. There will be others there.'

'That's fine by me.'

'You'd maybe like to join us, there's quite a crowd.'

Mayo's pulse raced. Had he found what he was seeking already?

'Our leader owns a house deep in the hills.'

'Tomorrow night then?'

'Fine. Make it late, after all the boozers have gone home and there's nobody about. Some way out of town there's a big island with a chocolate factory close by. Wait for me there. My name's Donna by the way.'

'I'll be there.'

'Marvellous, see you then.' With that she vanished back into the alleyway.

Mayo lit a cigarette, inhaled deeply. Events had moved faster than he had dared to expect. Where was Donna going to take him? That tumbledown house which Charlie Wells had referred to? Well, he would find out on the following night.

It was after 11 o'clock before Mayo started out on the long walk to the arranged meeting place with Donna. The night was dry and cold with the threat of a frost before morning.

He was reluctant to reveal either his accommodation or the whereabouts of his parked car. As far as Donna was concerned he was a drifter who had moved into the area like those drug dealers whom he had passed in the streets. Whatever the motive of those whom he was about to meet he would soon discover if they were allied to the master criminal whom Wells had mentioned. It was certainly going to be an interesting night. Instinctively he checked his .38, nestled in his pocket.

A somewhat battered Fiesta was parked just off the island. The headlights from a passing car revealed a girl with long fair hair sitting in the driving seat. Donna had arrived and was waiting for him.

'Hi there,' she leaned across, opened the door on the passenger side. 'Glad you decided to accompany me.'

'I wouldn't have missed it for the world,' he settled back in his seat. 'Where are we headed?'

'Just leave it to me,' she let in the clutch. 'We're going to have one helluva night. I believe that our esteemed Master will be paying us a rare visit. In some ways it's rather scary.'

'Oh?' Mayo was curious. Apparently, this was to be no ordinary gathering of those who were currently infiltrating this area. He was comforted by the weight of his handgun in his pocket.

She turned off the main road and the aging car shuddered under a steep climb on a single-track road. The headlights showed thick hedges on either side with sparse unkempt woodland beyond.

It was some time before she spoke. 'You're a strange one. Why do you wear that big hat?'

'It protects my head from the rain and wind and hot sun in summer.'

'Fair enough,' she laughed, then added, 'I'm going to Syria in a few days.'

'Oh?'

'To join the Al Qaeda Jihadists.'

'From what I've read in the papers they're fighting a losing battle, likely to be wiped out.'

'Nevertheless, I am going.'

'If you survive and are taken prisoner you are unlikely to be allowed to return to the UK, who will doubtless cancel your passport.'

'It's a chance I'm willing to take. And yourself?'

'I don't have any plans.'

She hesitated, slowed the car momentarily as they approached another bend in the pot-hole ridden road. 'What's your name?'

'Just call me John.'

'John, I'm... I'm scared.'

'Of going to Syria?'

'No... you see, our leader is visiting us tonight. He's a terrible man, even his own followers are frightened of him.'

'What's his name?'

'It sounds Russian to me,' she paused, 'Zinovsky.'

Mayo tensed, turned his head away in case his expression reflected by the headlights revealed his shocked surprise. 'Can't say I've ever heard of him,' he lied in a matter-of-fact tone.

'I've only ever seen him once before,' Donna's voice trembled. 'That was a year or more ago just after I had joined the group. He came to organise the setting up of the place. One of his top agents brought this tumbledown farmhouse and the land surrounding it. He was probably British, claiming to be a farmer. The place is virtually hidden by the surrounding wood and there are no rights of way so any walkers straying on it are trespassing and one of the guys living there tells them to sod off. You couldn't have a better place to get together and hide up.'

So, it wasn't the Farmhouse to which Wells had referred, instead another one so far unknown to the Department. Maybe a decoy also brought by this guy Zinovsky. If Williamson had discovered it then he had not been able to inform his employers. It was all decidedly sinister.

'Tell me more about this guy Zinovsky,' Mayo said, still with his face turned away from his young companion.

'God, the very look of him sends shivers down your spine,' she negotiated another sharp bend. 'Hunched body like he's deformed but it's his face which is so frightening. Like the flesh has wasted down to the bone but worst of all are his eyes, sunken deep in their socket, boring into you. They seem to glow. He's like... like I would expect Satan himself to look! And there are rumours that he has connections with the devil!'

'Stuff and nonsense!' Mayo grunted. 'I don't believe in any of this occult rubbish. It's an act put on to scare the living daylights out of folks.'

'Well *I* believe it,' her voice trembled. 'Our group is shit scared of him, as are others elsewhere in the world. There are stories which I'd prefer not to go into.'

'In which case I'll make my own mind up when I see him.'

'He's got an agent who checks on us regularly,' she continued, 'and he's enough to scare the shit out of you. He brings knives and pistols, bombs, too. Then he orders us to 'go out and kill'. I've known some of the group travel the length and breadth of the country to blow themselves up and as many citizens as possible with them. The cops have forestalled a good many but there's always the odd one which breaks through the net. I'll tell you this, John, before long we shall rule the world, civilization will no longer be as it is today!'

John Mayo did not reply. Donna had been radicalised sure enough. She had just one aim in her twisted thinking, to assist the jihadists in whatever way she could, even if she died doing so.

'Here we are,' Donna announced as they swung onto a rough tree-lined track and the headlights revealed a sizable stone house nestling in a hollow below. Donna parked her car alongside a Range Rover, switched off the engine and lights. 'It seems that Zinovsky has already arrived,' her voice trembled slightly. 'We'd better go in. Follow me.'

The house was sizable, built of stone sometime in the early twentieth century and in need of major restoration work. An unlit hallway led through to a sizable kitchen. The latter was crowded mostly with scruffy youths and around half a dozen teenage girls. The atmosphere was rank, a mixture of pot smoking and unwashed bodies. Heads turned to view the new entrants, but nobody spoke. There was a general sense of unease.

At the far end a raised platform had been erected with pallets, and on it stood a wizened figure whom Mayo had no difficulty in recognising from Donna's earlier description. *Leonid Zinovsky was in the process of addressing the gathering.*

Mayo tensed as the other's eyes centred on himself, sunken orbs that seemed to glow, a skull with withered flesh that had the appearance of rotting, a wide mouth with just a couple of teeth remaining.

'Another convert to our cause,' his voice crackled in the silence. '*There will be many more throughout the world. One of you,*' his gaze switched to Donna, and Mayo felt her clutching his arm; she was trembling. 'One of you is booked to travel to Syria in a couple of days. The news there is not good, the town of Baghouz is under heavy siege by forces from America, Britain and Europe. It is the final stronghold of Daesch, one of our most loyal Islamic State groups. Hundreds of civilians have either been killed or have fled. But we shall regroup, make no mistake about that. The enemy's victory is only a temporary one. Before long we shall rule the world. In the meantime, my message to you here is to go out and kill. We have a stock of knives, firearms and bombs. First, though, you must witness the fate which awaits our enemies who attempt to seek us out. Follow me.'

Zinovsky stepped down from the platform, shuffled towards another corridor at the end of the room, one that was dimly lit. At the far end was an open cellar door with rough steps leading downwards.

Mayo joined the throng, noted its atmosphere of fear. Donna's grip on his arm had tightened still further. His other hand gripped the .38 in his pocket, not that its six shots would be much good in this crowd. All the same it was comforting.

The onlookers huddled in the confined space of the damp cellar, its walls streaming with condensation.

That was when John Mayo drew in a sharp breath at the scene which greeted him, lit up by flickering candles.

Zinovsky stood to one side, bony fingers pointing to an inverted crucifix fixed to the stonework. On it was a human figure in torn clothing, still alive and moaning faintly with pain.

Mayo experienced a sense of nausea; Donna buried her face against him. He stared in horror and disbelief at the inverted crucifix, the victim's hands and feet were crudely nailed to the wood of the cross, blood seeping from the wounds.

Zinovsky stood to one side, a gloating smile on his withered face. Spittle seeped from his stretched lips.

'One who almost infiltrated this small coven of true believers,' his voice was a hiss now, a combination of anger and gloating. 'Our Master delivered him into our hands and now he must pay the supreme penalty!'

From beneath his cloak he produced a heavy bladed knife. He held it aloft for all to see and then, with one sweeping downward stroke, he slashed the crucified man's throat from ear to ear. Blood spurted, saturated the ripped clothing, dripped to the floor.

There were gasps from the audience, somewhere somebody was vomiting. A female screamed. The body shuddered and then became limp.

'Master, accept our offering of this traitor,' the executioner's voice was shrill. *'Others will follow, many will be slain on the streets, bombs will blow gatherings to a mulch of unrecognisable flesh and bone. Islam will rule the world!'*

Anger and revulsion seethed within John Mayo, his fingers gripped his handgun. He was tempted to destroy this vile leader of a growing revolution across the globe.

Then, suddenly, he recognised the bloody features of the man who had just died on that vile inverted crucifix. A shockwave that sent his whole body tensing, rigid. He recalled the photographs which Detective Inspector Wells had shown him.

The crucified body was none other than that of the missing Bill Williamson!

Chapter Three

A shriek of maniacal laughter came from Zinovsky, his heavy bladed knife uplifted in a bizarre salute to the crucifix and that which it represented. Amidst the gathering some were vomiting.

'Thanks to Satan who delivered this enemy of the Islamic State into our hands!' Zinovsky's cackle echoed in the packed cellar.

An uneasy fearful silence followed. His glowing eyes roved around his followers, finally settled on John Mayo who stood at the foot of the steps. An upraised hand, a claw-like finger beckoning. A summons.

The others pushed past the one who wore a black fedora, stumbling up the flight of broken steps in their terrified haste to be away from the scene of terrible death, until just Mayo and the slayer, along with his assistant, remained.

'What is your name? From whence have you come to the temple of jihadism?'

Mayo took a deep breath, squared his shoulders. This Devil from the dark must see that in no way was he afraid.

'I just drifted in, chanced to meet one of your followers who brought me here. I have spent months in London, a loner following your cause... until now when I decided it was time to move out elsewhere. By sheer chance I met Donna which is why I'm here now.'

'I could use a man like you,' Zinovsky's gaze dropped onto the bloody corpse behind him. 'You see what happens to our enemies!'

Mayo nodded. 'You need have no worries about myself.'

'Good. I have an important role awaiting somebody like you but to enrol your services in a scattered community like a rural Welsh town would be a waste of talent. These youngsters are doing a good job and Matthew,' he referred to his local organiser of this small cult who stood on the top step, 'is a fine ambassador for our cause. I have a special, much bigger, role to offer you.'

'I'm willing to consider it.'

'That is an excellent start. As you doubtless know our main activities are in London where there is a death most days, knifings, shootings, bombs. A few have been arrested but the police cannot cope. I am more than happy with the situation which is increasing daily. Second only to the capital is the West Midlands, almost five hundred slayings so far this year. Drug gangs work for us. However, we need somebody to oversee certain towns other than Walsall and Wolverhampton where major strikes would be a devastating blow to democracy. I refer to the city of Lichfield with its famous cathedral, Dr Johnson's birthplace, the former residence of Erasmus Darwin. I could go on, there are other major targets, all attracting visitors from the UK and abroad.'

'I see,' Mayo maintained a stoic expression. 'So what's my role to be?'

'We have a small group in the area but not sufficient to carry out the attacks where systematic multiple killings would bring an important community to its knees. Our man there, Richardson, has organised a cult of our followers but he is not up to major attacks. I will put you in contact with him, work with him. Our success there would be another major factor in destroying UK democracy.'

'I'll do my best,' John Mayo recognised an important role to be played on behalf of Counter Terrorism Command. He had already infiltrated the terrorists.

'Good. I will give you details of where to contact Richardson before I leave.'

It would have been all too easy for Mayo to have shot Zinovsky and his assistant there and then but it would not have solved the Lichfield situation. And, in any case, he would have been unlikely to have escaped alive from this hidden den of anarchists. Another time, there surely would be one.

Mayo became aware of a movement behind him. He had not heard the burly dark clad man, cloaked in a black gown, a hood partially covering pallid features, move from the shadows. The latter stepped down onto the floor and in his hand, Mayo saw a huge knife. He stood before Zinovsky clearly awaiting instructions.

'Get rid of this body,' a grunted order, a bony hand indicating the blood-soaked figure on the upturned cross.

'Yes, Master,' the other moved forward, began wrenching the victim's hands and feet from the woodwork so that the corpse crumpled into a heap. He bent forward and started sawing at the neck until the head rolled free, then moved onto an arm.

Mayo turned his head away, was close to spewing. His companion seemed oblivious of the gruesome amputations, began ascending the steps, motioning to Mayo to follow.

Upstairs in the kitchen, the group huddled in silence. Even for those who had already slaughtered innocent citizens on the streets this was too much for them.

'You have witnessed what happens to our enemies who fall into our hands,' Zinovsky addressed them in a gloating tone. 'Now I must be taking my leave of you.' He beckoned Mayo to one side. 'As I told you,' he lowered his voice, 'I will instruct you briefly on the role to which I am assigning you.'

'Sounds fine to me. I'll do my best.'

'It is important that you do. First you must travel to Lichfield and make yourself known to Richardson. I will advise him of your mission. Where are you staying here?'

'I've been sleeping rough,' the other lied, 'in a hay barn just beyond the town.'

'Needless to say you do not have vehicular transport.'

'No,' Mayo lied. 'I hitched a lift on three lorries up from London. I'll do the same to travel to Lichfield.'

'That will be fine,' Zinovsky's eyes narrowed, 'I am curious about your headgear…'

'I found it outside a second-hand clothing store so I took it. I fancied it.'

'A mobile phone?'

Mayo produced one, added 'I took it from a guy I attacked down in London. Don't worry I've fixed it so I cannot be traced by it.'

'Excellent. I shall be able to contact you when necessary.'

'By the way, is there any chance that I could take Donna, the girl who brought me here.'

'*No!*' A sharp reply. 'She goes to Syria shortly. Her nursing services are needed there.'

Mayo shrugged his shoulders.

'You are welcome to stay here tonight, though. There are ample sleeping arrangements,' his slit of a mouth twisted in what could only be interpreted as a grin. 'Use her for your enjoyment if you wish. It will be your only chance if that is what you have in mind.'

'I'll see.'

'Here are my contact details,' the other produced a folded slip of paper. 'Memorize them and then destroy this. Only Richardson has the means to contact me but you may wish to do so without his knowledge. He is a a devoted servant of the jihadist cause but I feel that the forthcoming plans for Lichfield are beyond his capabilities. I am relying on you.'

'I won't let you down.'

'You will forfeit your life if you do!'

Zinovsky's servant had completed his task, Williamson's body was a heap of bloody, barely recognisable joints. They were loaded into plastic fertilizer sacks. Mayo guessed that there was somewhere where they would be dumped, maybe a river far from here. He tried not to think about it

Shortly afterwards Zinovsky and his servant drove away. There was no mistaking the sense of relief amongst those remaining in the house as the drug addicts began smoking.

Mayo eased himself onto a vacant bed in the adjoining room, wrinkling his nose at the scent from the filthy blanket spread upon it. Clearly he had no option but to spend the night here.

* * *

Amidst the pervading odour of coffee being brewed in the kitchen came squeals of female delight. The horror of earlier in the evening appeared to have been forgotten after the departure of Zinovsky and his gruesome cargo.

Mayo removed his headgear, stretched his weary limbs. Maybe he would forgo that coffee at least for the moment.

Sometime later the door clicked open and a shaft of light revealed a female, her blouse undone, her long fair hair falling about her shoulders. There was no mistaking his surreptitious visitor. It was Donna.

'Hi, there,' a nervous whisper and a soft click as she closed the door behind her. 'I wondered where you'd got to, John. There's virtually an orgy going on back there, downstairs and upstairs, so I decided to keep out of the way.'

'Very sensible of you,' he was somewhat wary as she seated herself on the bed beside him. Wan moonlight streamed in through the un-curtained window. She was certainly a beautiful girl, cultured too.

'What a gruesome evening,' he grunted.

'Yes, but it has happened before,' her slim fingers were unfastening her jeans.

'Do you realise the implications of going to Syria? Daesch is experiencing heavy bombing from the allied forces. Many have been killed, others have fled. It will be wiped to the ground very soon.'

'I was training to be a nurse,' she eased her jeans down further and Mayo noted that she was not wearing underwear. 'I have a duty to tend the wounded to the best of my ability.'

'And get blown to smithereens along with hundreds of jihadists.'

'I have to take my chance on survival. I have a duty to perform to our followers.'

'Why don't you leave here with me? We could creep out tonight.'

'No!' she snapped. 'Our leader would find me, or rather his devoted followers would. You saw what happened tonight. I would suffer the same fate as a traitor to our cause.'

He sighed. They had radicalised Donna and nobody would change that, not even himself.

She stood up, shrugged herself out of the rest of her garments, sank back onto the bed naked. 'We never got round to it, John,' her fingers were starting to undo his own clothing.

'It was prostitution,' he whispered.

'Yes, but only to find another follower to our cause. You were already one of us as it turned out so now sex is purely for pleasure. God, I want it badly, John.'

He could have pushed her away but already an erection was starting. His thoughts flitted briefly to Gwenda but he dismissed them. Infidelity had been part of his career over the years. This time would be no different.

Now they were both naked, embracing, their fingers exploring each other's body. Her thighs opened wide, she was warm and moist between them. Her hand slid onto his hardness, began rubbing it softly.

Then she was up on her knees, her legs spread wide, guiding him where she wanted him, a slow penetration which brought gasps of delight from her.

God, it was fantastic, Mayo pushed upwards as Donna bore down on him, twisting and turning, grunting their delight. Then it was all over; she sank down upon him and they rolled over in an embrace. Shortly afterwards he dozed, slept.

Mayo awoke shortly before daylight. He was aware that she no longer lay beside him. She had left some time during the night.

He stirred, picked up his fallen garments and dressed. The adjoining room was silent, clearly the night of debauchery was over and the others slept.

It was time to be gone. He tiptoed through the kitchen, turned the key in the outside door and stepped out into the cool of the early morning. It was going to be a long walk, he quickened his pace along the narrow road back towards the town.

Donna was back somewhere in that remote farmhouse; he had abandoned the idea of trying to persuade her to join him. She would go to Syria, probably never to return to Britain. So be it, he had another mission to accomplish. He pushed all else from his mind. He was ready for whatever the future held.

Chapter Four

Having booked out of his temporary accommodation, John Mayo collected his car and began the long drive to Lichfield. Already he was formulating a plan in his mind. He would leave his car at the home of some retired farmers, friends from the past. Then he would make his way on foot to the city, another drifter from afar like those who were moving into the area and make his acquaintance with Richardson. After that he would play it by ear as was his usual mode when on a mission.

It was late in the afternoon before he arrived at the address which Zinovsky had given him. It was a sizable semi-detached house in a suburban street, one which blended in with those on either side and opposite. He crossed the road, tapped on the door. It opened almost immediately.

'You must be John Mayo. I was expecting you. Come inside.'

Mayo judged Dave Richardson to be in his mid-thirties, unkempt from his tousled hair down to his worn, dirty trainers. His eyes were sunken, his nose had been broken at some stage and two front teeth were missing. An unwashed odour emanating from him combined with a stench which could only be the result of smoking pot.

Mayo followed him through to the adjoining room which was cluttered with all manner of rubbish.

'Zinovsky has sent you to help me organise what is planned,' there was a note of resentment in the other's voice. 'Not that I need it, but a helping hand would not come amiss.'

'I'm happy to help with whatever you have got planned'.

'Fine, then I'd better fill you in. One thing I'll make clear at the start is that I'm in charge here and I will do the organising of our plans. That said, you could be useful.'

'Fair enough.'

'Good, now let me explain our forthcoming plans. We are in a prime position to deliver a devastating blow to the community here. Many other followers have moved in from the West Midlands principally Walsall and Wolverhampton. Some use this house as their residence, others are sleeping rough. More will follow.'

'Sounds fine to me. Where do I stay?'

'Right here so that we are in contact the whole time. There is a small room at the top of the stairs which you can use. I believe it was once a nursery when the former owners lived here.'

'So, what are the plans, Dave?'

Richardson motioned towards a frayed and dusty armchair. 'Move that clutter and sit down.'

Mayo deposited a pile of old newspapers and torn wrappings onto the floor. Christ, this was one hell of a dump, screened from the street outside by frayed curtains.

'The so-called Spring Bank Holiday is but a week away,' Richardson leaned back in an opposite chair, entwined his fingers, closed his eyes as if in deep meditation. 'That will be our Big Day when we shall strike a decisive blow against those who control Britain. For them time is running out. We shall bring them to their knees. ISIS will rule. Before long the countries of Europe will follow. Zinovsky is already amassing his followers. Mayo's expression was stoic, did not reveal his innermost thoughts.

'Our first major blow on the forthcoming Spring Bank Holiday Monday, that is the date for the so-called Greenhill Bower. It begins with the mayor crowning the Bower Queen on the steps of the Guildhall. Then a sizable procession begins, kids on lorries, tractors pulling other displays on a round trip of the city.

'People come from the surrounding district, the pavements are crowded. Alongside this is a large market in Market Street. Then there is the cathedral, always a big draw and crowded. In all there are thousands of visitors in the city, a prime occasion to kill hundreds.'

'I get you,' Mayo checked his rising hate and anger towards these mass murderers.

'A couple of bombs, one in the cathedral and another in the market which will also account for those visiting the nearby birthplace and museum of Dr Johnson.'

'How will you set it all up?' John Mayo asked.

'We have at least two prospective suicide bombers eager to sacrifice their lives in our cause. They can't wait.' He gave a laugh.

'And how do I figure in this?'

'A couple of drug gangs have moved into the city in recent weeks. They will be useful to us but there is a deadly rivalry between them. I fully expect a shooting or a knifing on the streets any night. We need to incorporate them into our cause. That will be your first task, Mayo, to make contact with them and work on radicalisation.'

'How do I go about it?'

'You will need to get out there at night, wait for a pusher to contact you. Buy some dope off him, talk to him. Beware, there is a limited police presence in the city looking for pushers. The last thing we need is a gangland murder which will only serve to increase those limited police activities. If you can contact the leader before that happens and bring them here, we will amalgamate them in our growing numbers.'

'Okay,' Mayo nodded. 'First of all, I need a rest after my long journey. Then I'll make a start after dark tonight.'

'There is a small room on the landing which I have already put at your disposal. Make sure though, that you are not followed here after your excursions. A small group of incomers from the

Midlands are already staying in this house. Zinovsky has arranged it all, bought this house under an assumed name. He has visited on a couple of occasions.' There was no mistaking the flicker of fear on Richardson's face.

'As you probably know we have already made contact in Wales.'

'So I understand. He has unlimited power throughout both Britain and Europe, and it is believed that he also has Russian contacts. And…' and the other grimaced, 'it is believed that he is also involved in satanism!' Richardson paled visibly.

'So I believe,' Mayo did not elaborate on the recent crucifixion.

'Then I wish you luck tonight,' Richardson straightened up out of his chair, delved in his pockets and produced a key. 'Here's a key to the door so you can come and go as you please.'

'Thanks. Now I'll go up and try and get some rest.' His body ached after the long walk from the distant farm but his brain was racing after the recent pep talk.

He mounted the stairs and as he reached the landing a door opposite the room which he had been delegated opened and closed, obviously a toilet. A young girl clad in flimsy night attire and with long dark hair falling about her shoulders emerged. Her attractive features registered a momentary surprise at seeing him.

'Hi!' She smiled briefly before opening the door of an adjacent room and disappearing inside it.

John Mayer stiffened as recognition suddenly dawned on him. He recalled that photograph which Detective Inspector Wells had shown him.

It was incredible, there was no doubt in his mind that the young girl was none other than Gemma Jones who had vanished from her Welsh home a few weeks ago!

Chapter Five

Mayo slept fitfully, awoke when street lighting began filtering into the room through the frayed and moth-eaten curtains. He had not undressed and instinctively he checked on the .38 handgun in his pocket. Alongside it was the crucifix which he usually wore around his neck, dangling inside his dark shirt. On this occasion he would keep it out of sight for it would be sheer foolishness to let these people see it for their mindset was clearly focused on the black arts.

There was no hurry. He lay listening, there were sounds of movement from other parts of the house. Then silence.

God it was stuffy in here, a lingering scent of pot smoking. In all probability the windows were never opened.

It was time to go. A match around the side streets, his dark clothing would render him almost invisible in the shadows.

He let himself out into the dimly lit side street, locked the door behind him. In the distance he heard sounds of revelry, late night drinkers returning home from the pubs. He moved on, using darkened doorways to stand and listen.

A patrolling police car passed by, disappeared into an adjoining street. The last thing he needed was contact with the law.

He started as a woman stepped out in front of him from a dark passageway. She was plump, middle-aged and had a pockmarked face.

'I'll do it for a fiver,' she dribbled as she spoke. 'A stand-up job against the wall.' She was already starting to unbutton her blouse.

Mayo did not reply, quickened his pace. He was on the point of deciding to return to his base when, without warning, a black clad figure wearing a balaclava, leaped out of the shadows. A heavy bladed knife was thrust within an inch of his throat.

'Mobile! Money!' His attacker grunted in shrill tones.

Mayo, shocked as he was, stood his ground.

'Come on or you get your fucking throat slit!'

John Mayo made as though to fumble in his pocket and then, too swift for the eye to follow, his right hand shot up and his fingers closed around that weapon-threatening wrist, thrust it away from himself. In the same movement his hand twisted with every ounce of force he could muster. It was followed by a sharp crack and the blade dropped to the pavement, clattered as it spun on the paving stone.

His attacker gave a sharp cry of pain, tried to kick out but the man in the black fedora was already standing on that foot.

'Now,' Mayo banged his attacker's head against the adjacent wall and ripped the balaclava clear of the features which it had masked, 'let's have a proper look at you, you bastard!'

The glow from a nearby streetlight revealed youthful features twisted in agony and shock. Another cry of pain. 'Let me go... please!'

'Not until we've had a little chat. You picked the wrong victim, sonny. What's your name?'

'My mates will kill you for this,' he was trembling, his voice was now a whine.

'Your name!'

'Martin... Martin Smith.'

'Where do you hang out? I guarantee you're not a local.'

'I... I come from Walsall,' the youth moaned with pain. 'There are several of us. They... they sent me to spy on any immigrants, a mosque maybe.'

'Neo-Nazis undoubtedly.' He gave the broken wrist another twist. The youth moaned. 'Which group?'

'National Action.'

A far-right organisation banned in the UK around five years ago. 'How many of them?'

'A dozen. They're part of a larger group who will join them when they get the word.'

'I know full well you scum are planning a race war,' Mayo's lips were tight, his expression revealed the hatred building up inside him. 'You're racist, anti-Semitic and homophobic, rejecting democracy, violent towards ethnic minorities. I've seen some of your propaganda material on social media before it was removed. You scum!'

The youth was crying with pain and terror. Mayo dragged him further into the shadows.

'Now I want details of where your mates are skulking.'

'Alright. If you'll let me go.'

'That remains to be seen.' He had confidence in his acute memory, he did not need to write the address down. It came in faltering tones.

'They'll kill me for this if they ever get to know.'

Mayo bent down and in one sweeping movement picked up the heavy kitchen knife. 'Right, on your way,' he turned, strode down the side street, crossed the city centre until he came to the small railing-enclosed stretch of water known as the Minster Pool. A splash followed as the knife disappeared, had a flock of mallard quacking in alarm.

Only then did he make a call on his mobile to Charles Wells. It was answered with a recorded message, doubtless the other had retired for the night.

Mayo gave the address in Walsall, adding, 'They're a National Action group. Raid 'em. A drop in the ocean but it's a start. Nothing to do with this jihadi business. I'm working on that. Leave it to me.'

Wells would act, Mayo had no doubt about that. Meantime he had to try to stop the proposed city centre bombing on the forthcoming Spring

Bank Holiday Monday. Massacres were looming on two fronts with death threatening hundreds of innocent citizens.

Chapter Six

'How did it go last night?' Richardson entered the small room where Mayo was staying. The latter had just returned from the kitchen downstairs where he had made himself a bacon sandwich. Food had been laid out on the table and it was apparent that you just helped yourself to whatever took your fancy.

'Very quiet', Mayo answered with a full mouth. 'Drinkers going home from the pubs and one or two whores looking for business.'

'It's early days yet. By the way I heard on the radio this morning that Daesch has finally fallen to the allies. A temporary setback for us. Zinovsky will drum up another force.'

Mayo nodded. He wondered whether or not Donna would be going out to Syria now. 'By the way, who's the girl in the room opposite?'

'Her name is Gemma, Gemma Jones. She came up here from Wales. She will be useful to us, I have no doubt. By the way, she's a good screw,' he gave a laugh. 'I've shagged her a couple of times, all part of the radicalisation process! Try her if she takes your fancy.'

'Maybe.'

'By the way, I'm expecting a delivery today. Bombs. A couple. All ready for the Spring Bank Holiday. A big 'un to be smuggled close to the cathedral and the small one for young Watkins to blow himself up, and hopefully a number of people in the market at the same time. The bombs are coming already primed so all we have to do is to hide the big 'un near the cathedral and make sure Watkins does his stuff at a time to coincide with its detonation. The cathedral bomb has to be snuggled up there which won't be easy with the tight security they have in force there. So I think that's a job for you and me, John.'

Mayo pursed his lips, nodded his agreement. It couldn't have worked out better. Already a plan was formulating in his mind.

'I'm going into the city later to do some shopping for myself,' he announced as casually as he could. 'Cigarettes and one or two other things I'm running short of.'

'That's ok by me.' Richardson cocked his head to one side. 'I think I hear a vehicle pulling up outside. That will be the delivery I was telling you about, the bombs. Follow me.'

Outside a somewhat dilapidated, small van was parked up against the kerb. The worn lettering on the side stated that it belonged to 'W. Johnson, Decorator'. The occupant wearing soiled denims and a frayed cap had just vacated the driver's seat.

'That's Williamson, at least that's what he calls himself,' Richardson muttered to Mayo. 'He was up here the other week delivering some firearms and ammunition.'

The man who called himself Williamson nodded to the others. 'A couple of boxes for you, doubtless you've been expecting them.' He moved to the rear of the vehicle, unlocked the double doors. 'They're not particularly heavy, you can manage to carry one each.' Which meant that he was not coming indoors. 'I've got to get back to London. Another delivery.'

The cartons were fastened with strong brown tape partly obscuring some labels which stated that they had once contained biscuits from a wholesaler. Mayo lifted the heavier and larger one, Richardson took the other.

'Our leader will doubtless be checking on their safe arrival,' the man was already moving back to the cab. He had no intention of prolonging his call. 'I'll see you next time there's a delivery,' he slammed the door as he spoke, started the engine.

Richardson carried the smaller container, Mayo followed him indoors with the larger, through the main room to a smaller one at the rear, the door of which the former unlocked. It was lit by a small bulb in the ceiling which revealed a shelf wall containing numerous boxes.

'Our armoury,' Richardson explained, 'all stocked for the day when the uprising begins.'

On a lower shelf was a selection of knives, large ones of the general household variety, their blades glinting where they had been honed to razor sharpness.

'Let's have a look at these bombs,' the smaller of the two men produced a penknife. 'We need to familiarise ourselves with their working before they are put into operation.'

Both were of metal construction, the larger one cased in a flimsy container with wires and an instrument panel. The lid of the main container had a simple switch to open and close it. Richardson clicked it back, lifted the lid to reveal tightly packed flaked material.

'I don't know what type of explosive it is,' he stated. 'I'm not versed in the details but we set this panel here to a date and time and that should do the trick. The most difficult part will be hiding it close to the cathedral, their security is top-notch. We'll have to make a visit along with all the sightseers first, work out how we're going to do it. It won't be easy.'

The smaller of the two bombs was cylindrical and had a belt attached to it. 'That's for strapping around the waist,' Richardson stated the obvious. 'Then all the guy carrying it has to do is to press that switch and hey presto he and those in close proximity will be blown to smithereens!' There was a small catch which opened the device, somewhat nervously he flipped it back. The interior was packed with the same pale coloured flakes of high explosive. He snapped the lid closed, let out a deep sigh.

'I'm glad we're working together,' there was no mistaking the relief in Richardson's voice. 'The setting up of the cathedral bomb will be the most tricky part. As I said we'll have to sense it out first and then work out how we're going to do it.'

'That's fine by me.'

'Oh, and just a thought. In case anything should happen to me I'll give you the spare key to the armoury. We can't afford any slip-ups. Now, you're going into town to do some shopping so I'll leave you to it. D' you think it's wise to walk around in that garb wearing that big hat in broad daylight?'

'I think it could be advantageous in the long run,' Mayo replied. 'I will probably draw a few curious glances from Joe public but these gangs who have moved in may well see me as a prospective ally. After all, we've got to get as many of them as possible working with us. So if they see me in the daytime they may well make contact after dark, just a thought.'

'I'll leave it up to you, John.'

Shortly afterwards John Mayo set off for town. Already a plan to fail the proposed Spring Bank Holiday massacre was germinating in his mind. The fate of hundreds of innocent people was at stake.

Chapter Seven

Mayo did not hurry, sauntered down the wide streets until he reached the city centre. The shops were busy, there was a queue at the butchers.

He was aware of curious sidelong glances from those around him. His shrewd gaze flicked over those he passed. There was no sign of any who might have belonged to the drug gangs which were moving into the area, at least none who were recognisable as such. They were lying low by day, would emerge after dark.

He bought some cigarettes, then entered a shop which offered an array of general goods for the average householder, umbrellas, and various containers for the kitchen. His searching gaze picked out a selection of shopping bags in all sizes for the convenience of the housewife. He moved to examine these, and found that which he was seeking, a large vinyl one that would accommodate a sizable purchase at a supermarket. He bought it and moved on.

A pet shop offered everything which the animal owner might need, dog and cat food of innumerable brands, dog leads of all types and lengths, a selection of rubber bones and other toys.

'Can I help you, sir?' An assistant came from behind the counter.

'Yes, I'd like some cat litter of the clumping variety, a sizable bag, if you've got one, or two smaller bags.' Mayo held up his recently purchased shopping bag. 'I'll carry it in this.'

'Ah, this will suit you, sir,' the other lifted up a 10kg sack, eased it into the bag which Mayo held open. 'Have you far to carry it?'

'My car's not far away,' Mayo lied. 'I'll be fine.'

He left the shop, set off on the long walk back to his temporary base. On the way, he paused at a convenience store, purchased some packet of biscuits, enough to hide the contents of his heavy shopping bag.

Fortunately, on his return there was no sign of either Richardson nor the other occupants of the house. He entered his small room, pushed his recent buy beneath the bed. Only then did he let out a sigh of relief. His mission had been successful, the next stage would be more tricky. He stretched out on the bed, relaxed.

Sometime later the door creaked open. It was Richardson who stood there, a strained expression on his scrawny features. 'Done your shopping?' he grunted.

'Yes, just a few things I needed.'

'Zinovsky called me whilst you were away. He was just checking that the bombs had arrived safely. And one other thing,' Richardson grimaced, 'he is coming here for the Spring Bank Holiday. He wants to witness the devastation, multiple deaths. I half expected it.'

'Well, he doesn't bother me.'

'Not right now because you're useful to him. But one mistake and you'll end up crucified like that copper. And don't forget, he has connections with Satan!'

'I'll bear it in mind.'

'Anyway, tomorrow we'll have a walk up to the cathedral, see where we can hide the bomb. That will be the trickiest bit.'

'I'm sure we'll manage.'

With the approach of evening, Mayo retired to his room, stretched out on his makeshift bed. There were around a dozen others in residence, he could hear their voices from downstairs, an aroma drifting up from the pot smokers.

It could be a long wait before he put the next part of his plan into action. He relaxed, there was no hurry. He heard Richardson mounting the stairs, his footsteps along the adjacent passage as he made his way to his room to retire for the night.

More movements downstairs as some of the others headed for their sleeping quarters. He wondered about Gemma Jones; there was no sound from the opposite room. Hopefully she was asleep.

Finally, he made a move, crept out of his abode, tiptoed downstairs. The main room was empty.

He returned upstairs, dragged the heavy shopping bag out from beneath his bed. He experienced a fleeting sense of tension, the last thing he needed was to meet one of the others.

Back downstairs he headed through the smoke-filled kitchen to the door of the 'armoury'. He felt in his pocket to reassure himself that he still had the spare key to the door. In his other pocket his handgun nestled, if he was discovered then he would have no alternative but to use it.

He unlocked the door, closed it after him and switched on the light. On the shelf in front of him were the two boxes containing the bombs. He extracted the larger one first, placed it on a nearby packing case.

He paused, listening. Silence.

He withdrew the small fastener and lifted the lid, viewed the flaked contents. A sigh of relief because to some extent they resembled the cat litter in the bag at his feet. There were several empty cardboard boxes in a pile under the shelving, he selected one, opened it and carefully poured the contents of the bomb into it. That done, he replaced them with the pet products, pouring slowly and carefully until the device was filled. He clicked the catch shut and gave a sigh of relief and satisfaction as he placed it back on the shelf.

The smaller bomb followed suit. That done he put the remnants of the litter back in the shopping bag followed by the explosive material.

His first step was completed. He opened the door, switched off the light and locked up. On tiptoe, Mayo returned to his abode and hid the bag beneath the bed. On his next nocturnal roam, he would smuggle it out and dispose of it in a place of safety. In all probability, anyway, it would be harmless away from the connection within the originated containers.

Hardly had he stretched out on his bed when he heard the door immediately opposite click and crack open. Doubtless that was Gemma Jones needing the loo at the far end of the passage. He had not so much as glimpsed her for days. In all probability she had sought refuge in her room now suddenly finding the present rough company not to her liking. Maybe her original dream was turning sour.

Now what? He drew a deep breath, let it out slowly. There was a pause and then the door creaked open. The light on the landing revealed what was clearly a very nervous Gemma Jones, her mousy coloured hair uncombed, a dressing gown draped around her thin figure.

'I'm... I'm sorry to disturb you,' she spoke in a whisper, 'but I was wondering if… if we could have a chat… I need to talk to somebody and… and you're not like that lot here… nor

Richardson.' She glanced behind her as if she feared that the latter might suddenly appear.

'Come inside,' John Mayo swung his legs on to the floor, 'and close the door behind you.'

There was an uneasy pause, she stood there wringing her hands together, looked up and down the landing.

'Well,' Mayo broke the silence, 'you don't need to be afraid of me. How can I help you?'

'I… I,' Gemma stepped into the room, clicked the door shut behind her. 'I'm very much afraid, Mister Mayo.'

'Call me John. Well you'd better tell me all about it.'

'I've been very foolish,' she licked her lips nervously. 'I… I didn't realise what all this was about. It sounded great, overthrowing those who rule the UK, make all the laws, tread on the ordinary folk. Richardson has tried to radicalise me but I hate him for it. I don't want any part in mass murder. He boasted that they are planning to blow up the cathedral, and a suicide bomber into the crowds on Market Street on the Spring Bank Holiday. John… I want to go back to my home in Wales.'

'Then why don't you just scarper after dark when everybody's asleep?'

They'd find me, hunt me down,' she was close to tears. 'I know too much. They would kill me.'

'What's your name?' The last thing he wanted her to know was that MI5 had her on file, had shown him a photograph of her.

'Gemma, Gemma Jones.'

'How old are you, Gemma?'

'Twenty last birthday.'

'I see. Well, maybe I can help you. I think we can work together.'

'You're different from the rest of this scum, John.'

'Many thanks, that's a big compliment. I just drifted in here and Zinovsky wants me to assist Richardson.'

'He's a bastard. He… he's already raped me.' Her voice trembled, she was close to tears. 'Is… is there any way you can help me. I just want to go back to my folks.'

'Maybe,' he stroked his chin, became deep in thought. 'Tell you what, there's no reason why we shouldn't have met as your room is opposite to mine. He wants us to have a nosey around the cathedral, look for somewhere this bomb can be hidden. I reckon if you came with us we could create a family appearance as far as the security blokes are concerned. You know, dad and daughter, Richardson an uncle accompanying us.'

'Urgh! So what do we do? I don't want to be part of mass murder.'

'Could you trust me? I'm not one of them in the true sense. Just a hanger on.'

'But Zinovsky has chosen you to assist Richardson in mass murder!'

'That's how it seems. If I said it won't happen would you believe me? But I am not going into details. Just accompany us on reconnaissance of the cathedral and leave it at that for now.'

'All right,' she nodded. 'I'll go along with you.'

'Good. I will fix it with Richardson.'

The following morning dawned warm and sunny. Richardson was already in the kitchen area along with half a dozen bleary eyed youths when Mayo went down.

'I guess we can do a recce of the cathedral today,' the other looked up. 'Best if you don't wear that big hat and draw attention to yourself. I'll find you another.'

'Fair enough. By the way, I've been making some plans. We don't want to draw attention to ourselves, so I've been chatting to Gemma. She's agreeable to accompany us. With luck we'll be passed off as father and daughter accompanied by an uncle. That way we won't arouse suspicion.'

'Hmm,' Richardson looked thoughtful. 'Well, maybe it's a good idea. I'm working on Gemma, she's becoming radicalised, one of us. I shagged her; you wouldn't believe it but in her early twenties she was still a virgin!' He sniggered. 'No more, I reckon that fuck was a turning point in her life. She's no longer mummy's little darling, like us she wants to see the UK overthrown, under jihadist rule.'

Mayo disguised his revulsion. What a bastard Richardson was!

'This right-wing lot have got to be wiped out,' the other continued. 'Nazis and jihadists will never mix even though both hate democracy. Zinovsky is working on that, along with Hamza bin Laden, so he told me the last time he was up here.'

Mayo nodded. 'He's got the right idea.'

'Too true. And don't forget that he's a Satanist. The Master will guide him. There's going to be some corpses and,' he sniggered, 'body parts littering the streets before this is over.'

'We'd better make a move,' Mayo's appetite for breakfast had waned. 'I'll go and get Gemma.'

Chapter Eight

Mid-morning saw the trio trudging through the side streets towards the city centre. Richardson led the way with Gemma and Mayo at his heels. The latter had exchanged his fedora for a somewhat worn cap which had been loaned to him. He retained his jacket and trousers, after all some of the shoppers wore black jeans and dark tops.

In Market Street, Richardson paused to survey the scene of the proposed smaller bomb.

'Ali Amani, that's the slim guy with the broken nose,' he spoke to his companions in a low voice, 'has volunteered to blow himself up amidst the crowds.' He gave a short laugh. 'A really dedicated member of our lot. I shall miss him but it's all in a good cause.'

Mayo glanced behind him, viewed the towering statue of the famous Dr Johnson on the cobbled square. On the opposite side of the street was the great man's birthplace, a house which has now become a Museum. History as well as lives would be destroyed if the proposed explosion went ahead.

They walked alongside the Minster Pool. Mallard and half a dozen Canada geese were resting on the water, quacking and honking contentedly. The Cathedral Close was crowded, tourists taking photographs and admiring the magnificent edifice. People were entering and leaving through the wide open doorway.

'What's going on there?' Mayo halted, watched a group of workmen clad in overalls hacking with pickaxes at the slab walkway to the left. A sizable heap of broken paving stones was piled up nearby.

'Looks like they're renewing the broken slabs,' Richardson answered. 'Just in case the visitors trip over.'

'Let's take a closer look,' Mayo moved ahead of his companions.

A couple of labourers struggled to extricate another slab, heaved it onto the sizable heap of extricated ones.

'Warm work,' Mayo spoke casually to the nearest worker.

'You can say that again,' the labourer mopped his brow with a soiled handkerchief. 'This should have been done weeks ago. The bloody clergy are worried about somebody tripping over, breaking an arm or leg and suing them. We've got to replace these with this lot before the holiday,' he indicated a couple of piles of replacements. 'They can't collect the rubbish until after the holiday so there'll be a heap of smashed slabs on every photo the visitors take. Still, that's not our worry.'

'Anyway, you're doing a fine job,' John Mayo moved away.

'Well, we'd better go inside,' Richardson was already moving towards the entrance.

'We don't need to,' Mayo halted him in his tracks.

'But... but we've got to look for a suitable hiding place for the big one.'

'We don't need to. I've already found it and you couldn't have a better one. It makes our job much easier and far less risky. Those broken slabs are excellent cover.'

'I'm going to relax by the Pool for an hour or so,' Mayo announced as they left the crowded Cathedral Close. 'I need a breather in the fresh air.'

'Well, I've got work to do,' Richardson announced. 'There's a very promising youth joining us. One of our contacts is bringing him over from Dudley. He could be very useful to us on our next mission.'

'Which is?'

'Zinovsky will inform me when he is ready to do so and not until. Doubtless it's somewhere in this part of the Midlands. All he told me was that we will need a suicide bomber and this guy fits the bill after Ali has done his duty.'

'I would like to have a rest by the pool too,' Gemma announced nervously. 'I haven't had much in the way of fresh air since I came to Lichfield.'

'That's fine by me,' Mayo agreed.

Richardson's expression was doubtful. 'Well, so long as you're not missing all day. I wanted to have a long chat to you about the future. You have an important role to play in our plans after the bombing, Gemma.'

'We'll be back in an hour or two,' Mayo was swift to reply.

'Oh, well, all right. Then, John, we have to plan our placing of the bomb outside the cathedral and ensure that young Amani knows exactly what he has to do on the day. It is vital that both bombs explode simultaneously. We don't want the crowd running for cover at the first explosion.'

'I'm confused,' Gemma announced as she and Mayo found a spare bench overlooking the pool. The walkway alongside the railings was crowded. Holidaymakers were already converging on the city in advance of the forthcoming events.

'Doubtless you are,' Mayo lit a little cigarette. Already he was convinced of the other's integrity. She had found herself caught up in a terrifying situation from which there seemed no hope of escape. Until now. Her radicalisation had failed.

'But…' she was clearly very confused, 'you're... you're playing a role in this planned bombing. I don't understand.'

Mayo took a deep breath and let it out slowly. By now he was convinced that she had no wish to join a jihadist movement. All she wanted was to escape from this increasing bunch of murderers.

'I'd better explain,' his hand found hers, squeezed it. 'I'm going to trust you, and in return for your loyalty I'll help you to escape and rejoin your family. If I fail then we will both end up on the crucifix.'

'Alright,' she shuddered. 'I promise I won't betray you.'

He related the role he was playing, how he had rendered both bombs harmless. Once that was discovered his own life would be in danger. So he had to escape and he would take Gemma with him. Somehow also he had to kill Zinovsky, hit this movement where it hurt most.

'Now I understand,' she was clearly relieved. 'So where do we go from here? I'm dreading another session with Richardson.'

'Unfortunately, I can't do anything about that right now. But at least his radicalisation isn't working with you. Don't worry, after those bombs have failed to explode you and I will have got the hell out of here. I'll contact the Anti-Terrorism Branch and before these murderers know what's happening, they will be raided by an armed unit. Whether or not Zinovsky will still be there remains to be seen. If not, then I'll have to hunt him down before he leaves the UK. Right now, though, we better be getting back.'

Gemma's hand found Mayo's again, squeezed it. 'You've no idea how much better I feel now that you've put me in the picture.'

'Just hang on and everything will work out. Tomorrow night Richardson and myself go to place the cathedral bomb. After that it's in the lap of the Gods.'

Chapter Nine

It was after midnight when John Mayo and Richardson left the house. The latter carried the heavy bomb in a folded sack beneath his lightweight raincoat.

'The moonlight will be a big help,' Mayo remarked. 'At least we won't have to use a torch which might attract attention. Beware of patrolling cop cars, the last thing we want is to be stopped and searched.'

Richardson grunted. He was clearly nervous.

Twice they dodged into doorways when they saw headlights approaching from an adjacent street. A slow-moving police patrol car passed slowly by and then was lost to view.

Down along the railed path by the Minster Pool a couple were making love on the grass, grunting as they writhed. They were so engrossed that they did not even notice the two men pass by. A raft of mallard quacked loudly and in the trees on the opposite side an owl hooted. An omen.

Then they were in the Close, sneaking past the railed section of the roadway. Up ahead of them was St. Chad's Preparatory School; no lights showed, the boarding pupils had long retired to their dormitories.

Every few yards Mayo and Richardson stopped to listen. The night was silent, there was not a soul to be seen. Lights showed behind the curtains of a couple of residential homes.

'Couldn't be better,' Mayo whispered. 'Now, here's that pile of broken slabs. We'll need to lift a few off carefully so as to make no noise. You do that whilst I keep watch.'

Richardson removed a number of the slabs, made a space amidst those remaining. Then he carefully placed the bomb within it. He checked the tiny screen, moved the catch to set it. Then he replaced the residue above it, ensured that they resembled an untidy heap. Nobody would ever guess what it screened.

'Phew!' He straightened up. 'That's it. The bomb is hidden and all set. We'd better get back and hope for the best.'

They moved away, dodging the moonlit areas. A couple of those previously lighted bedroom windows in the houses opposite were now in darkness. The residents had clearly retired for the night.

'What's our next move?' Mayo asked as they made their way back alongside the Minster Pool.

'I now have to work on Ali Amani, make sure he knows exactly what he has to do. He's keen enough to blow himself up but we have to work out a plan for him. It is essential that his bomb and the one by the Cathedral detonate at exactly the same time, or within seconds of each other. We can't afford any slip ups especially with Zinovsky up here. Christ, that guy terrifies me just looking at him!'

Mayo did not reply.

Back at the house he went upstairs to his room. He listened, heard Richardson cross the landing, the latter's door clicking shut behind him. There was no sound from Gemma's bedroom. He would wait awhile. It was time for both of them to get the hell out of here.

It was in the early hours of the morning before John Mayo stirred, dressed fully, pulled the fedora down on his head. Then he tiptoed out onto the landing, eased Gemma's door open. By the moonlight streaming through a gap in the curtains he saw her lying on the bed.

She started, sat up in alarm. He held a finger up to his lips.

'What... what is it?' A whisper of undisguised alarm came from her. She clutched a sheet around her naked body.

'We're leaving,' he spoke in low tones. 'You'd better get dressed. I want us to be well away from here before Zinovsky arrives tomorrow.'

'Where are we going?' She fumbled with clothing, her hands shaking.

'Back to your parent's home in Wales for a start but we'll have to move on somewhere else from there because Zinovsky will try to track us after he discovers his bombs are dud's. First, though, we've got a long walk down to where I've got my car hidden.'

'It will be a relief to get away from here, John.'

She followed him out onto the landing and down the stairs. He unlocked the door and they stepped out into the warm, moonlit night. Only then did they quicken their pace down the deserted street. There was no sign of late night vehicles for which he was relieved.

It was over an hour before they reached the home of Mayo's friends. He saw his car parked in their driveway where he had left it. He was reluctant to disturb them but he could not chance them contacting the police next morning when they discovered it was no longer there.

Just a brief word with their bleary-eyed friend. No explanations, just that he was taking the car and would be in touch at a later date.

Minutes later John Mayo was driving away, Gemma Jones beside him in the passenger seat. After a short time, she drifted off to sleep. She had finally relaxed, perhaps for the first time since she had left her family home.

Dawn had started to creep over the eastern sky by the time they reached Rhayder. On the extremity of this township Mayo turned off onto the mountain road which led to Aberystwyth.

'Approaching home territory,' Gemma had both relief and excitement in her voice.

They did not see any other vehicles as they travelled the narrow winding mountain road. 'My folks live at Cwmystwyth,' she announced. 'That's a tiny village a few miles outside Devil's

Bridge. It's in a hollow amidst what's left of the slate mining from a century or more ago. Remote except for a never-ending stream of coastal traffic in the summer months.'

'I'll pull in and we'll wait a while before knocking your folks up. Seeing you back home will be a shock enough for them. But you and your parents will need to make plans to move elsewhere for a while. Richardson knows where your family home is and that's the first place they'll come looking for you. And me.'

'Why should they bother, John?'

'Because you know too much, the whereabouts of the Lichfield group for a start. As for myself, I'm going to hang around. Doubtless Zinovsky will blame me for the dud bombs. Then there's Ali Amani, he'll run yelling into the city centre and when his bomb fails to detonate, he'll be caught and interrogated. Things aren't looking good for that lot and Zinovsky will certainly want revenge. What he'll do to Richardson is anybody's guess,' he gave a humourless laugh. 'I'll tip off my contact and the Anti-Terrorism branch can carry out a raid. First, though, I shall be tuning into the radio for a report on this Lichfield business. Zinovsky won't just disappear from there before he comes looking for you. So I have to ensure that you and your folks are in a safe hideaway.

Me, I'll stick around the Cwmystwyth area. I might just get a crack at that bastard. He's reputed to have occult connections so there's no knowing what his next move will be.'

Mayo parked up opposite the small white-washed house which had been Gemma's home since childhood. It stood back from the road, surrounded by a lawn and neatly maintained borders. Close at the rear was woodland which stretched up the steep hillside beyond.

He knocked on the door, heard footsteps approaching and a key turning in the lock. An overweight woman, possibly in her late fifties with flecks of grey in her short auburn hair, glanced from Mayo to Gemma, stared in disbelief. A shriek of surprise and then she was embracing her daughter, crying.

'Oh, my darling, I don't believe it. You've come home!'

More footsteps and then a tall grey-haired man with a clipped moustache, braces over his short sleeve shirt appeared.

'I… I… Gemma!' He grasped the door post for support. His gaze settled on Mayo, curious and questioning.

'May we all come inside?' Mayo smiled. 'I think we need to have a chat.'

'I'll put the kettle on.' She led the way through the hall and into the neat and tidy kitchen.

'I'm John Mayo and I finally found your missing daughter.'

'I can hardly believe it,' Rodney Jones himself was close to tears. 'This is my wife, Martha. We've been calling the police every day in the hope that they might have some news of Gemma. We knew she had left to join those revolutionists and we had virtually given up hope of ever seeing her again. I can't thank you enough.'

'It isn't quite as simple as that,' Mayo leaned back in his chair and lit a cigarette. 'This is just the first move. They will come looking for her. And for me. First, though, something is going to happen, or to be more correct, not happen tomorrow in Lichfield. These guys will be enraged. They will want their revenge on myself as well as Gemma. Is there somewhere you could move in the meantime?'

'We have a close friend, a widow, who lives at Abbeycwmhir on the outskirts of Rhayder not far from the Elan Valley. She bought a piece of land there some time ago, erected a mobile home on it to live in whilst a bungalow was being built for her. She has just moved into her permanent home but the mobile home is still waiting to be taken down. Cath is a lovely lady, and I've no doubt she would be only too happy for Rod, Gemma and myself to move in there. What are your plans then, Mister Mayo?'

'I shall remain here. I'm hoping that Zinovsky, who runs this vile set up both in the UK and Europe, will accompany his confederates and provide me with the opportunity to destroy them once and for all!'

'Oh, my goodness!' Martha Jones clasped her hand to her mouth, Gemma clutched her mother. Rodney pursed his lips.

'We can certainly arrange it, I'm sure,' the latter stated. 'If you think it is really necessary, Mister Mayo.'

'Call me John. Yes, I'm certain that it is. Tomorrow is Bank Holiday Monday. I would like you to have left here by early afternoon because that is when the events will happen over in Lichfield which will enrage Zinovsky.'

'I'll give Cath a ring right now,' Martha rose from the table, went through to the hallway.

'I can never thank you enough for finding Gemma and bringing her home, John,' Rodney's voice trembled.

'Once she saw what society was up against, she was shocked. It's far from over but with luck I can hit 'em hard. There's a camp at Roj crammed with thousands of refugees, some citizens who have survived the conceited attack by the Allies but also a huge number of jihadists waiting to reorganize and hit back. I just wish I could get Hamza bin Laden in my sights but I guess that's too much to hope for. Anyway, as I said I'll stick around here and I'll tune into the radio tomorrow afternoon and see if there are any reports from Lichfield. Zinovsky's in for one helluva shock and my guess is he'll put two and two together and realise that I scarpered with your daughter, and the first place he'll look is here!'

Chapter Ten

Zinovsky arrived at the Lichfield base late on the night of the eve of Bank Holiday Monday. He was accompanied by his nameless lieutenant, dressed in black clothing, a cloth balaclava masking most of his cruel features. An expert at crucifixion and other types of torture, he stood behind his master as the latter addressed the gathering in the large room.

Richardson was clearly nervous, his tongue licking his lips and fidgeting with his hands by his side. Ali Amani stood at the front of the group, an expression of maniacal pride on his dark features, relishing the major role which he would be playing the following day. Heroic death was but a change, he would live again in another world.

'Are the bombs primed and ready?' Zinovsky addressed Richardson.

'Yes, everything is set as instructed.'

'Excellent. We are all aware of the fate of Notre-Dame cathedral in Paris. Arson? An electrical fault? Whatever, the Master has played a part in that, his powers are beyond human comprehension. Now the cathedral in this city will suffer a similar fate. Hundreds will die both there and in the crowded streets.' He fixed his gaze on Amani. 'Behold we have a devoted follower and hero in our midst.'

Amani smiled, his eyes glazed over. He was relishing his role. He would live again amidst those who had sacrificed themselves in the cause.

Zinovsky's expression changed, his deep sunken eyes scanned the gathering. Searching for a familiar face, not finding it.

'Where is Mayo?' A harsh, demanding question, his gaze centred on Richardson. 'And the Welsh girl?'

'He's somewhere out on the streets, hoping to find others to join us. I presume the girl is with him.'

'I see,' Zinovsky's suspicion was only too obvious, 'but why has the girl gone with him?'

'I… I…' the other had no logical explanation. Maybe Mayo and Gemma were starting an affair and that could be disastrous to future plans. 'Just companionship, a breath of fresh air for Gemma maybe.'

'She'll be headed to Roj soon. They need all the help with the sick and wounded they can get. I want some answers from both of them when they get back. Now, to plan for the morrow…'

Richardson licked his dry lips. Pray that nothing goes wrong. Zinovsky did not tolerate failure.

'We shall remain here, we shall hear the explosion in the city. The cathedral bomb is timed for 1 p.m. and the moment you hear it, Amani, you detonate yours. The crowds will have no warning. Dead and wounded will litter the streets!'

Ali Amani nodded, muttered 'I am delighted to die for our cause.'

'Excellent. Now I suggest that everybody get some rest. My companion and I will rest awhile here awaiting the return of Mayo and the girl. They have some questions to answer.'

The gathering broke up, shuffled away to their respective nocturnal rooms. There was no mistaking their unease. All of them were nervous both of Zinovsky's presence and whatever the morrow held.

John Mayo watched the departure of Gemma and her parents. Dawn was already lighting up the eastern sky and the day promised to be another scorcher.

He smiled to himself. Zinovsky and his followers would be in for a big shock by early afternoon. Once they discovered that their bombs were duds they would be after him with fury and vengeance in their black hearts. He would be ready for them. Instinctively his fingers crossed over the handgun in his pocket.

Lichfield was packed to capacity with visitors from far and near. Crowds thronged the cathedral, a long queue forming at the west entrance. Security was tight with memories of the Notre Dame disaster still fresh in everybody's mind. A freak accident but following on had been the terrible bombings of worshippers in Sri Lanka and Nejombo and Colombo.

Back at the Guildhall the mayor was crowning the Carnival Queen. The market in Market Street was busy and there was a queue at the doorway of the adjacent Dr Johnson's house.

On the outskirts the terrorists grouped outside their hideout, waiting, listening for the cathedral clock to strike the hour. Zinovsky's expression was stoic, he rarely revealed his thoughts except on those occasions when an uncontrollable rage possessed him. He glanced at his watch, in just a few more minutes all hell would be let loose. His Dark Master would see to that just as he had done on previous occasions.

Back in the marketplace Ali Amani lingered, a suicide bomber relishing the outcome of the small bomb secreted beneath his denim jacket, finger and thumb on the detonator. He was trembling in every limb with excitement. The blast would blow him to a better life.

A trio of armed police were in evidence, the presence primarily to reassure the public of their safety. They did not anticipate any trouble. All the same they shouldered Heckler and Koch MP5 9mm submachine guns with 30-capacity magazines as well as holstered handguns. If the need to open fire in a crowded environment arose then it was safer to use the latter.

Their eyes roved up and down the street. If danger threatened then they were primed to spot it before there was a disaster.

Amani was waiting for the distant clock to clang its single note which would echo over the city. That was when he would break into a run, screaming abuse before he littered the street with dead and dying innocents. His only regret was that he would not be able to view the mangled corpses and hear the screams of the wounded. Or would he?

Clang! The single note from the clock in the Close vibrated, seemed to echo a note of doom which hung in the hot atmosphere.

Ali Amani broke into a run, sent a young mother sprawling headlong, overturning the pram she was pushing and catapulting a six month old baby onto the pavement. Shoving people to one side, screaming insanely he pulled the detonator on his bomb.

'Die you fucking bastards!'

A police officer standing in a nearby doorway acted with lightning speed devoid of panic. His handgun was drawn, instantly aligned on his target, a headshot. The report was deafening, then drowned by the screams of those around him.

Amani was dead, killed in full flight, rearing upwards and then falling back, sprawling in the roadway, arms and legs splayed, the bomb bouncing and rolling, coming to a halt against the kerb.

'Take cover!' the officer yelled. *'Get off the street!'*

People pushed and shoved their way into nearby shops. Panicking crowds stumbled down towards Dr Johnson's house and into the adjacent street opposite, screaming, dragging children with them.

The officer surveyed the open space around the sprawled corpse. He had expected the nearby bomb to explode. It still might.

Holstering his handgun, he made an urgent call on his radio. Two more uniformed police joined him.

'It didn't go off!' one of them remarked in faltering tones.

'It still might. Clear the street. The explosive experts and an ambulance are on their way.'

The cathedral clock was silent. In the distance was a babble of voices. Tourists further away were totally unaware of what had happened. The carnival procession was already beginning in the adjacent street.

A major disaster had been averted.

Chapter Eleven

'Something has gone wrong!' Zinovsky's near skeletal features reflected both puzzlement and rage. From the house they had heard the distant clock strike. Then, almost immediately after, the crisp report of what was undoubtedly a gunshot. People were screaming.

'Well?' He turned on the frightened Richardson. 'No explosions. And Mayo and the girl have not returned. What has happened? Why has Amani's bomb not exploded?'

Richardson was trembling violently. 'I... I… can't explain. The cathedral bomb was all set to explode at one o'clock. Maybe Amani held back waiting for it.'

'Then what was that shot? Why are people screaming when there has clearly been no death and destruction? Is this something to do with Mayo?'

Zinovsky was shaking with rage. Those around him cowered.

'Tonight, after dark, you and I will go up to the cathedral and find the bomb... if it is still there!'

Richardson nodded.

'In the meantime, we must wait.'

From afar came the wailing of police and ambulance sirens. The screams had died away. Whatever happened in the city, the incident had been concluded.

Forensic experts advanced on the bomb lying in the gutter. They risked death but it was their duty, somebody had to check the device and render it harmless.

One of them bent down, opened the container. He flipped the trigger catch on it to its safety position, breathed a sigh of relief. Then he opened it, stared in shock surprise at its contents.

'This stuff isn't explosive!' He turned towards his companion. 'As far as I can make out it's some kind of harmless shit! What the hell is all this about?'

Behind them the body of Ali Amani was being loaded into the ambulance. It would be taken away for a detailed analysis of the cause of death and identification. There could well be clues on the body and clothing which might lead them to the perpetrators of this crime. Likewise, it could be just a stupid hoax by one who merely sought to create terror. The truth would come out in the near future.

Another police car arrived. A detective superintendent from the local force addressed the officers. 'Clear the street and close the road,' he ordered. 'Shut all the shops. A thorough search and investigation must commence at once.'

The harmless 'bomb' had not succeeded in ruining the carnival and spoiling the enjoyment of a host of visitors in this ancient city.

Midnight was long past before Zinovsky and Richardson set out towards the cathedral. People were still about which on this occasion was an advantage. It was easy to mingle with late night drinkers without arousing suspicion.

Richardson was terrified of what they might find or not find. Mayo was clearly a traitor to their cause who had slunk into their midst. He had fooled Zinovsky from the outset which was unbelievable. Even Satan's disciple had not suspected him of being a traitor.

Underlying Richardson's terror of his companion was the worrying thought that the man in the black fedora might be planning further moves against them. Was he a police officer, an undercover agent?

'Here we are,' Richardson announced in a whisper as they slunk back into the shadows by the cathedral entrance. There was nobody about because there had been no indication of the hidden danger. The huge ornate doors were securely locked and in the wan moonlight the row of carved gargoyles above seemed to leer down on the two intruders into their domain. He could not repress a shiver which ran up his spine. He was shaking in every limb. 'It's in that heap of broken paving stones.'

'Get it out!' A hissed command. 'We will take it back to examine it. We cannot chance being discovered here.'

Richardson struggled to lift the heavy rubble. His hands were scratched and bleeding by the time he had uncovered the bomb. A sigh of relief that it was still there escaped his lips. With shaking fingers, he flicked the upper trigger into a safety position.

He was aware of Zinovsky's eyes boring into him, they appeared to glow in the enshrouding shadows; it was probably his imagination. He lowered it into the bag in which they carried it here. Then began the trek back, Richardson breathing heavily under the weight of his cumbersome cargo.

Back at the house there was no sign of the others, they were sleeping off the latest traumatic experience and they certainly did not want to be around when the feared Zinovsky returned.

Zinovsky led the way through to the small armoury. 'Open up!' A clipped order.

Richardson's fingers shook as he fitted the key in the lock. His fear was that if the other was made aware that he had given Mayo the spare key then it would evoke an outburst. Right now, there was no need to confess to it.

Once inside with the bomb placed upon a packing case Zinovsky's near skeletal hand opened it up, exposed the contents.

'This isn't any kind of explosive!' He snarled as he ran the flaky contents through his fingers. *'This bomb's a dud!'*

'I... I... wouldn't know.'

That was when Zinovsky's gaze dropped to the floor, stared at a scattering of the contents close to the doorway. A gasp of surprise merged into fury.

'Look, it's over there by the door. But it didn't come from when we opened this. It was filled before and by somebody who swapped the charge for this stuff and spilled some as he left. *You've replaced the charge with some harmless substance, Richardson!*'

'No, no, I swear it was not me!' He was panicking, heaved at the stench from his companion's foul breath as Zinovsky's rising rage reached a peak.

'Who else, then, could have done it?'

'It... it must've been Mayo.'

'Impossible, the door was locked.'

'I... I gave him the spare key. Just in case something happened to me.'

'*You... you what*!' Zinovsky's response was a piercing screech as his fury erupted. An outstretched ice-cold hand closed around Richardson's neck, slammed his head back against the wall. Those deep sunken eyes glowed red, the stretched mouth became a bestial snarl, spittle dribbling down his chin.

'So, Mayo sneaked in here, swapped the explosive for some harmless substance, probably in that of the suicide bomb, too. He's been working against us from the day he arrived on the scene and now he's fled, taking that girl with him. But he has not escaped, that I vow. Do you know where her folks live, where she came from to join us?'

'Yes, yes. It's a house in Wales, in the mountains close to Aberystwyth. It's called…' he paused, 'Cwmystwyth.'

'Then we go there, right away, in your car, Richardson. And when we find them, they will die, slowly and painfully. Have you ever carried out a satanic crucifixion?'

'No… never!' The other was close to fainting.

'Then this will be your initiation to one. And I personally will hack off the tenderest parts of their bodies whilst they still live. Their screams will be music in our ears! My faithful companion will oversee it, but you will carry out the mutilations!'

Chapter Twelve

The bank holiday dawned, warm and sunny. After Gemma and her parents had departed for the temporary residence Mayo sat outside the front of the house in a deck chair and attempted to relax. Nothing would be happening until later in the day, probably not until tomorrow when Zinovsky had discovered that his bombs had been tampered with. That was when all hell would be let loose. For sure he would come here seeking a terrible revenge.

He closed his eyes, attempted to relax. That was when memories of his past life intruded his thoughts. They always did, he would never ever dispel them for good.

He was no stranger to the city of Lichfield; he had been a special agent many years ago on the trail of an international assassin. He had concluded his mission satisfactorily and that was when he had met Penny, fallen in love and they had moved in and lived together. Marriage was a strong possibility but one Sunday morning she had complained of a violent headache which he had presumed was a migraine. She had retired to bed but when he had checked on her a few hours later she was dead. It had not been a migraine as he had presumed, instead a fatal cerebral attack.

The memory still brought tears to his eyes along with a sense of guilt. If only...

Now he had Gwenda and they were very much in love. All the same his past haunted him.

His thoughts turned again to those days in 1988 when he was working for an organisation dubbed Operation Werewolf, an anti-terrorist force which was under the control of Charlie Wells, a young man then in his first role on that scene.

Wells had sympathized with Mayo after the latter's loss and ordered him to take a break for a week or two. 'Go where you choose, try to relax,' he had said. 'Come back when you're ready. There's no rush.'

Mayo's wanderings had taken him to Knighton, a small town on the Shropshire / Welsh border. His intention had been to relax but it had not turned out like that.

The inhabitants were living in a state of fear. There were rumoured to be vampires in the locality, an ancient legend becoming reality.

Mayo's investigations had revealed a small terrorist organisation which he had eventually destroyed.

Now fate had decreed that he was up against the largest terrorist force in the world, under the leadership of Zinovsky who was in cahoots with Hamza bin Laden. There were others, a hate preacher named Zahran Hashim had been named as the alleged mastermind behind other massacres. He had been calling for Islamic superiority and the destruction worldwide of democracy.

Right now though, Zinovsky was Mayo's main target. Destroy him and it would be a major setback for the terrorists.

Mayo dozed, plagued by memories of the past and fear for the future of Britain and Europe. Already there had been major massacres.

A few hours later he tuned into the news on his radio. He tensed as he heard a brief report of that which had occurred in Lichfield earlier.

'This afternoon a suicide bomber was shot dead by police in Market Street, Lichfield. Mercifully the bomb was not detonated and has been taken away for investigations along with the body. The street remains closed. However, the carnival was able to continue in other parts of the city. We hope to have a full report of the incident at a later stage.'

Mayo smiled to himself, heaved a sigh of relief. His ruse had worked so far. No details were given of the smaller bomber, they would probably be announced on the following day. The cathedral bomb was clearly still in that pile of broken concrete slabs. Zinovsky would attempt to retrieve it and discover the problem but he would not be able to do that until well after dark when the crowds were gone. Then he would be headed for Cwmystwyth, the destination supplied by Richardson.

All of which had Mayo several hours in which to prepare for the terrorist leader's arrival.

He lit a cigarette, watched the evening sky darken. The full moon was waning but there would be moonlight later, enough to reveal details of his surroundings.

It would be foolish to remain indoors; they could well firebomb the building, drive him out to the hail of gunfire. No, they would seek to capture him alive, submit him to a similar fate to that of Williamson, another counter-terrorist command undercover agent.

He needed to move his car elsewhere. In addition to revealing his presence here they could well damage it. There was a farm a short distance down the road just outside the scattered village with some barns.

He drove down, found the farmer, an exceedingly friendly man, in the yard.

'That's fine by me, mister. There's plenty of room in the barn, leave it there.'

Mayo explained that he was staying in the Jones's residence for a few days whilst they were away on a short holiday.

Step one completed, he gathered up a couple of blankets from the bedroom. Tonight, he would have to maintain a vigil outdoors, the steeply sloping woodland provided an ideal vantage place.

Dusk was creeping up the narrow valley as he stepped outside, locked the door behind him. It was then that a movement up on the edge of the wood attracted his attention. Something rustled the ferns. A sheep from those grazing further along? No, it was too big, much darker in colour. Momentarily it was hidden from his view. What the hell was it?

Bracken moved and seconds later the animal appeared in full view. Now there was no mistaking it's breed; *it was a fully grown wild boar!*

Mayo stared in disbelief. Then he recalled a recent report that these creatures had infiltrated Wales. Recently, a sow and several young piglets had also appeared on Cannock Chase just a few miles from Lichfield. These had been rounded up and transferred to a farm.

The UK population of boar was increasing at an alarming rate. Numbers were such in the Forest of Dean that in spite of culls by the forestry commission they were spreading out into the countryside, moving to fresh habitats. Along with this there had been illegal releases from breeding farms by animal rights activists.

Wild boar were re-inhabiting the UK after having been eliminated around three centuries ago. Secretive, elusive animals they mostly emerged from their chosen woodlands after dark to feed and decimate farm crops and grazing land. They would never be eradicated.

Ramblers were advised to be wary. Mostly, boar slunk into cover at the approach of humans but a sow with young could launch an attack, especially if walkers had dogs with them.

Up on the hillside, beyond the cottage, that animal had emerged into the open, only just visible in the gathering dusk. Its very stance was one of defiance, staring down at Mayo, watching his every move. Incredibly It had sensed his presence here.

He wished that he had a powerful rifle to hand. His handgun would be worse than useless if he tried to shoot the boar; a wounding which would only serve to infuriate it.

'Damnation!' He spoke his frustration aloud. 'I daren't stay indoors tonight as there's every chance Zinovsky and his gang will turn up and firebomb the place and now there's a bloody wild boar out there!'

It was still up there, motionless, defiantly watching the cottage in the gathering gloom. There was something about its very posture, its head thrust forward in an aggressive manner which was somewhat disconcerting, like it had singled Mayo out, contemplating a charge if the opportunity arose.

Mayo moved back indoors. Maybe it would become bored and depart. All the same its presence was somewhat disconcerting. Like some supernatural power had sent it here.

After all, Zinovsky was reputed to be a disciple of Satan…

Chapter Thirteen

Richardson was trembling as he slid into the driving seat of Zinovsky's car, a black Ford Kuga Titanium X. They were joined by the latter's henchman, still wearing his dark cloak and balaclava. He did not speak a word.

Richardson wondered why this guy was not behind the wheel, instead sitting bolt upright on the rear seat. Both his companions made him fearful, ruthless men who would not hesitate to commit murder in the most bizarre and disgusting way.

Now Richardson regretted his role in this entire setup. Christ, why on earth had he confessed to giving Mayo a spare key to the armoury? He could have shrugged it off, suggested that the man in black must have picked the lock. Yet he had learnt that lying to their leader was a waste of time, those sunken orbs bored into you, virtually burning the truth out of you. One dared not lie to him, he was truly a disciple of Satan.

Even now Richardson was scared of what his own ultimate fate might be. His only hope was to appease his master in whatever transpired tonight.

God, it stank in here, a putrid odour which came from Zinovsky, a stench akin to rotting human flesh. He heaved, only prevented himself from vomiting with a determined effort. He swallowed the bile which had risen in his throat. Even its taste reminded him of a decaying corpse.

It was cold too, like being out of doors on a frosty winter's night instead of a balmy summer one. Like the overpowering stench, he knew that it came from his passenger.

Jesus, he had a three-hour drive in front of him. Somehow, he had managed to set the sat nav for Rhayader, he knew that by turning off there on the mountain road it would take them straight to their destination. And what then? He preferred not to think about it.

There was little in the way of traffic on the road, something for which Richardson was grateful. Even so driving was not easy when he was virtually shaking with fear. On one occasion he hit the nearside kerb, the impact shaking the car.

'Fool!' It was the first time Zinovsky had spoken since they had left Lichfield, his tone reflecting his seething anger over Richardson giving Mayo the opportunity to foil their double plot.

He brought the car back under control, muttered an unintelligible apology for his error. Mile after mile, not exceeding 40mph. If a problem had materialised, he knew he could not have coped with it, but he consoled himself with the thought that satanic powers were not likely to encounter such a trivial happening.

Rhayader. Up ahead the headlights revealed a right turn. Now they were on the mountain road, serene and beautiful in the wan moonlight but also terrifying for Richardson in its loneliness.

He had already convinced himself that before this night was over he would die. It was the mode of death which scared him the most.

A sharp bend before the road sloped steeply downhill. Another misjudgement, the rear side wheels bumping on the grass verge. Zinovsky's lurch forward was held by the extremity of his seatbelt. An unintelligible curse, a blast of putrid breath which enveloped the driver. The wheels bounced along soft grass until they returned to the tarmac. The rear passenger was cursing, too, his teeth grinding.

'If that happens again,' Zinovsky's eyes seemed to glow like coals in a smouldering fire as he thrust his near skeletal face towards Richardson, 'Baghdadi will drive because you will no longer be with us. Come dawn, the crow's will be feasting on your flesh!'

Richardson shuddered, the name was only too familiar to him, that of a leader of the Islamic State terrorist network who had been reported killed in Mosul, Iraq, some 5 years ago. Had he somehow secretly survived or was he another of the living dead?

Richardson's sweaty hands gripped the steering wheel. He slowed to 30mph. He could not afford another mistake.

Cwmystwyth. A road sign announced that they had arrived at their destination. Standing well back from the road on their right, a whitewashed cottage shone serenely in the moonlight.

'Drive on and find a parking space off the road, preferably screened by trees,' Zinovsky's order was terse like he, too, was feeling the mounting tension within the car. 'Then, hopefully we will take those in that house by surprise. I want Mayo and the girl alive. They must suffer before they die!'

Chapter Fourteen

The bar of the Devil's Bridge Hotel was packed to capacity with tourists. Set on the main road to Aberystwyth it overlooked a steep valley with the river below, a favourite haunt of Walkers who wanted to explore the sheer beauty of this place, a haven for wildlife.

In the far corner of the large bar room a young couple relaxed after a tiring trek in the mountains. Adrian Chambers had recently been made redundant from his job in the Birmingham car industry. Tall with tousled fair hair and of muscular build, he was in his late twenties. The loss of his job which he had had since leaving school had come as something of a shock. All the same he opted for a redundancy payment rather than a transfer to another factory. He would not be sorry to leave the city with its high rate of air pollution and non-stop crawling traffic emitting dense fumes.

So he decided to take a short break, loaded his car with camping equipment and his barbeque and headed for the Welsh mountains.

On a visit to Aberystwyth he had met Louise whilst relaxing on the crowded beach. Petite with short dark hair, she had recently broken off from her boyfriend and, like himself, was taking a break from her home in Dudley in an attempt to reorganise her life. She had no intention of returning to her job as a boring shop assistant.

Thus, they had much in common, lying on the warm sand and chatting. Towards early evening he had asked her if she fancied going for a drink with him.

'That would be nice,' was her instant reply.

'Let's go back up the valley,' he suggested, 'to Devil's Bridge. There's a nice hotel there.'

'Fine' she smiled and began folding up her towel. 'I really could do with a complete change.'

On the way back to his parked car his hand found hers. Her fingers squeezed his. His pulse raced.

They found a vacant table in the corner of the bar room and sipped wine in an uneasy silence.

'What are your plans now you've left your job and don't fancy returning to the Midlands?' he asked at length.

Louise shrugged her shoulders. 'I've no real plans right now,' she answered. 'I came up on the train and I've booked in at a B&B at Borth. I'll have to give some thought to the future, maybe find a holiday job for the summer and then see where I go from there.'

'Much the same with me,' he glanced out of the window, dusk was already creeping in. 'Have you eaten today?'

'Just a sandwich.'

'Same here. Tell you what,' he hesitated, 'I've got my barbecue in the car and some burgers. How do you fancy a moonlight barbeque up in the hills? It's a warm night and we could sit and admire the moonlight view of the valley.'

'Sounds great!' Her reply was instant. He refrained from adding that they could camp up there. He would suggest that later. Right now, his pulse was racing.

Half an hour later found them parked up past the old slate workings where the woodlands began. There was a well-worn track leading uphill. He hoisted the barbecue under his arm, gave Louise the carrier bag of food to carry.

It was a lengthy trek but eventually they reached the open moorland. Below, the winding river sparkled in the moonlight.

'Fantastic!' Louise breathed, sat down in the heather to regain her breath. 'This really was a splendid idea of yours.'

He busied himself setting up the barbecue on a small area of level dry heather.

'Beef, pork or chicken?' he asked, slicing some rolls.

'Chicken, please.'

Before long an appetising aroma wafted and they were sitting eating, each with their own thoughts.

'God, I'm tired.' She laid back, stretched.

'Same here.' He lowered himself down beside her.

Behind them, the coals in the barbecue were glowing red, sparking in the faint breeze.

Before long, his lips found hers and received a responsive lingering kiss.

'I could go and fetch the tent,' he stated.

'It's a warm night,' she wriggled her body up against his own. 'Let's relax, we can always go back later.'

His hand eased up her blouse, closed gently over a breast. She was not wearing a bra and the nipple between his fingers was hard and erect. She made no move to push him away, groaned softly as he undid the buttons on her blouse.

Now he was stroking both breasts, moving from one to the other. Her eyes were closed. He lowered his head, his tongue protruded, and he flicked it; her nipple hardened still further. His lips closed over one, sucked it, moved to the other.

Her whole body quivered; her head was back. Somewhat hesitantly he lifted her short skirt. Much to his surprise, and delight, he saw that she was not wearing any underwear. Her thighs moved, opened, and he viewed well-trimmed pubic hair which afforded him an unrestricted view of the soft pink flesh beneath. It was oozing moisture, warm to his touch.

He stroked it and then his probing finger penetrated her. A gasp of delight came from her. She was urging him on, desperate to go even further. She eased herself up so that he could slide her blouse off, followed by her skirt.

She was stark naked, her legs spread wide. That was when he reared up, removed his own clothing, cast it aside.

As he knelt between her legs, she lifted a hand, sought his throbbing erection and guided it down where she wanted it.

A slow penetration had her whimpering her delight, pushing herself at him until their pubics met. At first it was a slow thrusting, his member sliding back and forth bringing squeals of delight from her. Then they speeded it up and both were writhing in orgasms, touching each other, shuddering in the heather beneath them.

Finally, it subsided, and they lay there, kissing and murmuring how marvellous it had been. Adrian withdrew slowly, his erection softening but still she kept a hold on it.

'Can we go again?' she whispered, rubbing it.

'Shortly,' he replied. 'I'm sure I can make it again.'

Which he did. Then they were lying together, drowsy and slipping into an exotic sleep where togetherness predominated.

A warm breeze had begun to sweep the mountains, rustling the undergrowth. Behind Adrian and Louise the coals in the barbecue began to glow redly, some were sparkling. Then came a sudden gust of wind which fanned the embers, sent a small cloud of sparks into the air. They landed in the tinder, dry growth beneath, wisps of smoke coming from it, tiny flames taking hold, starting to spread in all directions.

Adrian and Louise slept on, his hand resting between her naked thighs, her fingers still encircling his limp organ. Then came the start of an erotic dream.

Behind and above them, flames from the displaced barbecue fire had taken hold, were leaping and spreading, crackling.

Adrian stirred, smelled smoke, coughed.

'What is it?' Louise relinquished her hold on him, sat up.

'I… I…' the crackling fire was growing by the second. *'The bloody hill's on fire!'*

He dragged her up onto her feet. Both stared in horror at the blaze which was rapidly devouring everything in its path, heading towards them. The heat was intense.

'We can't go back down the track,' there was panic in his voice. 'We'll have to go down through the woods, hope we can find a route. Come on!'

The naked pair fled towards the nearby trees at the area, heedless of the twigs and stones which gouged their feet. It was an awesome, terrifying sight behind them, they dared not look back at the pursuing inferno.

Running, stumbling. If it had not been a moonlit night they would have had no chance of making it to safety.

They emerged into a sizable clearing surrounded by bent and twisted silver birch trees, bright moonlight revealing every detail.

'There's a track leading out there,' Adrian pointed with one hand, held Louise tightly to him with the other. 'Let's go…'

His voice trailed off, something had moved out of the bracken opposite, a sizable animal. It was not one of the sheep which grazed these hills, it was far too big, and the wrong colour, black. Its head lowered, momentarily screened from them, until it reared up and stepped out into a clear patch of moonlight.

'What... whatever is it?' There was a hint of fear in Louise's voice.

'I… I… it's... it's a wild boar!'

The creature was stationary, head up raised as it regarded the two humans with eyes which reflected the moonlight and appeared to glow. Its posture was more than just curiosity. It was one of anger at those who had dared to trespass in its domain.

Adrian's mouth was dry. Behind them a raging fire was fast catching up with them, in front of them a fearsome animal of the wild barred their escape route.

'What... what are we going to do Adrian? Louise whispered, trembling.

'Well, if that fire catches us up, we'll be burnt to cinders,' his voice shook. 'So, I guess we have to chance that boar. I've read that they mostly avoid humans, just sneak away. Come on, we don't have any alternative.'

They walked forward hesitantly. Some thirty yards in front of them, the boar stood its ground. Clearly this one had no intention of slipping away and making itself scarce.

Then, without warning, it lowered its head and launched into a fast, lumbering charge.

Louise screamed. Adrian grabbed her around the waist, pulled her behind him, a futile effort to shield her. An instinctive glance on the ground at his feet, a hopeless search for a weapon of some kind but there was nothing. He shouted, waved his free arm, a useless gesture.

The boar had its head down, its huge tusks protruding, its feet drumming, faster and faster, a bundle of hate and fury for those two humans.

Bone cracked on bone, Adrian's leg broken instantly, throwing the pair of them down in a heap. Without slowing, it did an incredible turnabout for its size and then it was upon them.

Its tusks stabbed, penetrated tender flesh, dug deep. Blood spouted; more bones snapped. Louise's screams were silenced as her throat was torn open, Adrian's loins were gouged, penis and testicles catapulted into the air.

Silence apart from the snorting of the enraged beast. Then its head went down and its powerful jaws began to rip at the soft flesh, munching and slurping at the feast which it had been gifted in this lonely place.

Only when its hunger had been satisfied did it raise its blood soaked snout to the heavens as if thanking the dark gods for this gift.

Its nose wrinkled, it smelled the smoke from the advancing inferno, heard the crackling of blazing undergrowth. It was time to be gone.

It loped along a hidden track known only to itself and gambled downhill in the direction of Cwmystwyth.

Chapter Fifteen

John Mayo knew that it was time to be gone from the cottage. There was no doubt in his mind that Zinovsky and some of his companions would be arriving before dawn, enraged and seeking to vent a terrible revenge upon him for foiling the Lichfield massacres.

His .38 was in his pocket, loaded with silver bullets. His crucifix dangled from his neck down inside the dark shirt. Over his arm was a folded blanket for, wherever he stationed himself up there in the small wood, it would be bitterly cold even on a summer night.

He locked the door behind him for all the good it would do, possibly a delaying tactic. He pitied the Jones family for they would probably lose their lovely remote home before this night was over.

He arrived at the edge of the steep silver birch spinney, turned and looked back down on the white-washed cottage, clearly visible in the moonlight and the road beyond it.

Certainly, this was an excellent vantage point, no movement below would escape him. The only question was where to station himself. It was likely to be a long night. Maybe nothing untoward would happen. Of course it would, he reminded himself. By now Zinovsky would have discovered that the bomb planted by the cathedral had been rendered harmless and there would be no prizes for guessing who was responsible. His fury and desire for revenge would know no bounds. Richardson would give him the address of Gemma's Welsh home and that would be his first port of call.

A stunted oak tree, its branches twisted by gales over the years, grew on the fringe of the wood. Ideal, Mayo decided, the centre was no more than six feet above the ground, basket shaped and providing an ideal place to sit and wait. It offered a suitable view and he was safer up aloft if they came looking for him.

It took but a couple of minutes to haul himself aloft and then he settled down for a long wait. The atmosphere cooled as the night progressed, so he wrapped the blanket around himself. His handgun was within easy reach if it was needed. This time he would not hesitate to shoot Zinovsky. The building below was beyond the range of the .38 so he would need to wait until that vile perpetrator of unspeakable evil embarked upon a search of the immediate area. He could not afford to make a mistake and reminded himself that the other was reputed to have connections with the Dark Powers.

The night wore on. He listened for the sound of an approaching vehicle but not a single car passed along the distant road below. His vigil could well be a complete waste of time. All the same he did not relax for a moment.

Suddenly he detected a whiff of smoke in the atmosphere. It was coming from the western side of these mountains, obviously some distance away. A moorland fire? There had been several in the Welsh Hills since this spell of dry weather had begun. Most were started by the heat of the sun on a piece of broken glass. But not during the night hours. Arson?

If a raging moorland fire headed this way then Mayo knew that he would be forced to abandon his vigil and seek safety elsewhere.

Then he heard a movement some distance behind him in the woodlands, a rustling of the undergrowth, a crackling of fallen twigs on the ground. It could be a fox or maybe a deer which had smelled the smoke and was moving to a safer area. It was definitely heading in his direction.

It was impossible to discern anything in the darkness of this woodland. The rustling and cracking was intermittent like whatever animal it was preceded cautiously, stopping and listening every so often.

Suddenly a huge shape emerged some fifty yards to Mayo's left, only just discernible in the shadows cast by the trees behind it. It was big, certainly neither fox nor badger .... nor a deer. What the hell was it?

It moved out onto the open ground, now clearly visible in a shaft of moonlight. *It was a wild boar!*

Well, he supposed, it wasn't as strange as it might have been. There were wild boar in Wales and this one had obviously been inhabiting the uplands. That fire had obviously caused it to vacate its habitat.

The smell of burning in the air was stronger. If the fire was sweeping towards this place, then he would have no option but to vacate his vigil.

The boar had not moved away in the opposite direction as Mayo had anticipated. It was still there by the trees but now its head was uplifted and it was staring in his direction. It was creepy, a shiver ran up his spine. In effect he was trapped up in this tree. And how the hell did it know he was up here, it couldn't have scented him from that distance? It was most certainly watching him.

The creature remained motionless for several minutes and then it moved downhill in his direction. Slow, steady steps, heading directly for the tree in which he was perched. And all the time its head was uplifted, its hair-shrouded eyes glistening in the moonlight. Then it halted, barely twenty yards from him, its tail flicking from side to side. It's very presence, it's posture, was threatening like some supernatural power had sent it to find him. *And to kill him*!

An ally of Zinovsky's, a four-footed devil sent by the Dark Powers?

'Don't be so bloody stupid!' Mayo spoke aloud in an attempt to restore his confidence. He eased the .38 out of his pocket. Oh, God, how he wished that he had a rifle, a heavy .308. Yet his target was now somewhat nearer, his handgun might do the trick. He steadied it on his uplifted left arm, his proposed target needed to be above a front leg and just below the shoulder to achieve a heart shot. Move sideways, you bastard! It remained stationary just like it sensed his intention.

Somewhere in the far distance he heard the screaming of sirens. Fire engines. Doubtless the blaze had been seen and reported. *Good luck, chaps, just prevent it from spreading down here.*

A chest shot then if he was unable to obtain a side target. Or wait a little longer? He took a trigger pressure and just as he squeezed the boar leaped to one side with a speed which belied its size. Then it was bolting in the opposite direction. Seconds later it had vanished back into the wood.

Fuck it! Mayo ejected the spent shell. Well, at least he had got rid of the bastard! For the moment he would remain up here in safety, he was not going to take any risks.

The report from the shot seemed to echo across the hills for ages before it died away. Sirens were still wailing over yonder. And then he heard the sound of an approaching car on the road below.

It was some minutes before it came into view, creeping along slowly, the occupants obviously looking for their destination. It was without lights, the moon was bright enough for the driver to see the road. Mayo recognised it as a Ford Kuga Titanium X.

Zinovsky had arrived, the final confrontation was imminent. Mayo remained in his tree seat. If they came up here looking for him then the advantage was his. This time he would ensure that his aim was true.

Chapter Sixteen

'Pull over and park under those trees,' it was the first time Zinovsky had spoken since Richardson had bumped the grassy verge several miles back.

The driver swung the wheel over, eased the car into a space beneath some silver birch trees where it was screened from any passing motorists, not that there were likely to be any at this hour. He switched off the engine.

'Get out and don't slam the doors.' Richardson and the balaclava-clad backseat passenger obeyed. Zinovsky was already walking back in the direction of that remote white-washed cottage. He would doubtless reveal his plans when they were in sight of it.

Richardson's mouth was dry, his legs seemed scarcely able to keep up with his companions. He knew only too well that he was the fall guy now; he had a price to pay for allowing Mayo access to the armoury resulting in the failure of the bombs to explode back in Lichfield. There should have been mutilated corpses littering the front of a cathedral and around the marketplace. Instead the carnival had progressed with just the closure of one street and the death of a suicide bomber.

The trio surveyed the Jones's home from beneath a tree at the foot of the driveway. The sky to the west was lit up by a fiery glow. More sirens wailed.

'Our master has sent the fires of Hell to aid us in our quest,' there was a note of undisguised triumph in Zinovsky's whisper. 'It is a sign that we cannot fail. Now, Richardson, creep up and check if that building is occupied. We need to know if Mayo is in residence. If any of us have to die then it will be you! If he is in there then we must lure him out into the open. And that girl, who is the traitor to our cause, must also die. Slowly and painfully!

Richardson knew that he had no choice other than to check that cottage. Zinovsky had insisted that he had accompanied them unarmed. If Mayo killed him, so long as he had lured him from his refuge, then he would have served his purpose and paid the ultimate price for his foolishness.

'Get up there!' Zinovsky gave him a push. 'In all probability the place is locked up so observe through any windows where the curtains have not been closed or there is a gap. Listen for any movements or anything which might reveal Mayo's presence inside.'

Richardson's mouth was dry as he walked up towards the dwelling. He kept to the shadows on the side of the driveway. Behind him his companions were virtually invisible beneath a roadside tree, primed for the appearance of Mayo. They would probably opt for a wounding shot if he showed himself, just to disable him. Then would come his grisly death, together with Gemma. Doubtless she would be raped.

He reached the cottage, flattened himself against the wall, edged towards the nearest window. The curtains were closed. He shuffled on a couple more yards until he came to the front door. Dare he try the handle. Mayo might be waiting inside, ready to shoot whoever opened it.

No, he dared not risk it. He came to the end of the front wall. There was a side window here, the curtains were not closed. Hesitantly, fearfully, he risked a peep inside. In the semi-darkness he recognised a bedroom, everything neat and tidy. Clearly the bed had not been slept in, the coverlet unruffled.

He crept on, came to the rear of the building. A couple more windows afforded him a view of the interior. Once again there was no evidence of anybody. His cautious progress brought him back to the front. Dare he try the door handle? Arm outstretched, his back pressed against the wall, his shaking fingers closed over it. It did not move, the door was clearly locked. From the inside or outside? There was no way of telling. Unless Mayo was well hidden indoors then the cottage was unoccupied. If he had departed, then where had he gone? There was no sign of a vehicle so perhaps he had left the area, taken Gemma and her folks to an unknown place of safety. Richardson hoped so, for in that case it would avoid a confrontation.

Keeping to the shadows he made his way back to where the others were stationed.

'Well?' Zinovsky's whisper demanded a report.

'The place is empty. They've fled elsewhere.'

A frustrated intake of breath. 'They're not far away, I know. We'll have to search the wood up above.'

In the distance they heard further wailings of sirens. The firefighters had summoned help. The smell of smoke was now stronger.

'We'll get burned to cinders,' Richardson made the first excuse that came into his fearful mind.

'So will Mayo if he plans on hiding up there. He'll be forced to show himself.'

'Something… something's moving up there,' Richardson pointed. 'On the edge of the wood!' The trio stared. There was definitely a rustling of undergrowth and then a bulky, dark, furry animal emerged into a patch of moonlight.

It was the wild boar. It had not fled from the smoky atmosphere; it moved cautiously, wary after the shot which had almost claimed its life.

'*Our master has answered my plea for help*,' there was undisguised triumph in Zinovsky's voice. '*He has sent a fearsome creature to aid us in our search for Mayo. We must follow it, it will lead us to him! Keep your eye on it, Richardson, we are close behind you.*'

Which meant, Richardson concluded, that he was the fall guy. If Mayo was hiding out up here, he would take the first bullet whilst his companions dived for cover and returned the fire.

He stuttered on ahead of them. Once he caught his foot in a protruding tree root and fell face-down. Behind him, Zinovsky cursed.

The wild boar disappeared in the shadows. They waited and heard it again. Strangely it was heading in the direction of the fire from which it had previously come. Now it embarked upon a wide circle, lumbered back in their direction but was clearly keeping well clear of them.

'Strange,' Zinovsky muttered, 'either it does not want to go any nearer the fire or it has established that Mayo is not in this area.'

The creature was some fifty yards to their left, visible briefly when it crossed a patch of moonlight, but mostly they only had the cracking and rustling of the undergrowth to determine its position.

'The Dark Powers know best,' Zinovsky muttered. 'We can only follow in its wake, but right now the signs are that Mayo has fled from here.'

Up in his tree rest, Mayo had glimpsed the trio entering the wood further down. They were too distant for him to risk opening fire. Again, he glimpsed the boar up ahead of them. It most certainly knew where he was hidden but it was not risking another shot. Had it adapted the role of a hound leading its followers to him?

Now was the time to be vacating this eerie place whilst they were out of sight. As quietly as possible he descended to the ground. In the distance below he had witnessed Richardson checking the cottage, doubtless verifying that it was empty. In that case it would be the ideal place to take cover. His pursuers were unlikely to return there.

He dropped down onto the slope and, taking advantage of every scrap of darkness, made it safely to the cottage. He unlocked the door, entered and secured it behind him. Now, once again, it was a waiting game only this time the advantage was his. He stationed himself by the curtained window, pulled the folds apart slightly so that he could see outside. He eased the sash so that it would be possible to open the window swiftly.

Then, .38 in his hand, he sat and waited. This bizarre game of hide-and-seek was fast approaching its climax. Death awaited the losers.

Chapter Seventeen

The wild boar approached the tree in which Mayo had been hiding when he had shot at it, but this time it showed neither caution nor fear. Strangely it knew that he was no longer up there.

It stood there on the fringe of the wood, motionless, head thrust forward, bathed in a pool of moonlight. It was watching the trio of humans on the slope below.

Richardson was the first to become aware of the beast's presence, a stumble on the uneven ground had caused him to glance behind.

He stared in shock amazement. Was this yet another twist in this bizarre nocturnal hunt for John Mayo and Gemma? There was no mistaking its aggressive stance. An attempt has been made on its life, it seethed with a desire for revenge on any human.

'Look!' His cry was little more than a hoarse whisper.

The pair way below him, stopped, turned. Stared.

'*The creature sent by our master,*' Zinovsky breathed, '*to hunt down Mayo and the girl if they are hiding out up there. But it should not be returning here. Maybe because of the fire up there. Perhaps the Dark One has sent that, too, flames direct from hell!*'

Richardson was staggering, he had twisted an ankle on the uneven ground. He tried to regain his balance, lost it and sprawled headlong. On his hands and knees, he attempted to rise.

'Help me,' he called out but there was no response from those below. They were invisible in the shadows.

He sensed movements to his rear, a pounding followed by a kind of snorting.

'What... oh, God, no!'

It was that wild boar. It had come thundering down the slope and now stood only a couple of yards from him, tusks lowered menacingly.

He was helpless, unable to flee. The beast's eyes were fixed upon him, glowing. Watching him. If only Zinovsky had not demanded that he accompanied them unarmed he could have shot at it close range.

Bestial fury from hell itself. He managed a piercing scream and that was when the boar charged. Head lowered, its tusks gored into Richardson's abdomen, ripping his clothing and sinking deep into soft flesh. Blood sprayed; entrails were strewn all around. His bowels opened.

Still alive, his screams weakening by the second, he writhed beneath the fearsome onslaught. Chewing and slurping, the boar fed hungrily.

'It's got Richardson!' Zinovsky grunted. *'Something has gone wrong; it was sent by the Master to hunt down Mayo but now it seems that any humans are its prey!'*

Smoke billowed from their rear. The fire had swept down with unbelievable rabidity, devouring everything within its path. Only the cottage and the woodlands directly behind it were temporarily spared its ravages.

Sirens screamed further along the road as another contingent of firefighters arrived. There was no way Zinovsky and his companions could return to their parked car. They were trapped between that fearsome boar and the advancing fire.

Zinovsky offered up a silent plea to the Dark One. *Save us, Master, from a terrible fate.*

From the front window of the cottage, John Mayo had witnessed Richardson's fate. One down and two to go. He knew only too well that the one he sought to destroy was somewhere out there in the close proximity to his own refuge. It seemed that the still breeze had changed the course of the fire. Now it blazed between that farm up the road and his own refuge. The area of woodland behind might now be spared, for the moment it was the only place of safety, albeit temporarily.

Then in the moonlight, and only just visible through the drifting smoke, he glimpsed two figures scurrying uphill on the far side of the cottage. Like himself, Zinovsky and his henchman were seeking safety in the only area available to them.

Mayo knew that he had to go out there. He had no choice. The cottage itself was no longer a place of safety. How far that fire would travel was anybody's guess. Zinovsky and his henchman would be somewhere in the wood. If he could come upon them then he would destroy the one who was rallying the forces of evil throughout Europe and the UK in an attempt to overthrow democracy.

Unless they found him first. He had to embark upon a terrifying game of hide-and-seek with occult forces attempting to influence the outcome. It was the most fearsome challenge he had faced in all the years since he had been an agent of Counter Terrorism Command. A peaceful retirement with Gwenda over the past few years had been severely disrupted. If he was successful tonight then he promised himself that this would be his final mission.

Another glance down the hillside towards the road below. Richardson's mutilated corpse was strewn on the ground but there was no sign of the boar. It had killed and fed, moved on. In which direction had it gone? Was it back up there in the woodlands, maybe following Zinovsky and his companion or had it fled elsewhere, away from the raging fire? Mayo had no way of knowing. His .38 was in his hand, primed for a shot if the occasion arose against either man or beast.

He reached the fringe of the wood, crouched with his back to a tree, alert and listening. Over to the west, the sky reflected the flames of the moorland fire, a faint crackling as they devoured heather and gorse. There was neither sight nor sound of wildlife, fur and feather had long fled to safety elsewhere. Sirens no longer wailed, every emergency vehicle within a radius of several miles was already on the scene. Now that the wind direction had changed, the inferno would be on course for the massive slate quarries some distance away and would possibly burn itself out there where there was nothing inflammable to fuel it.

All of which left John Mayo and those he hunted in the smoke-filled small wood. His eyes watered, it was almost impossible to see in the smoky darkness which even the moonlight struggled to penetrate. He made an effort not to cough and reveal his presence. Strangely it was bitterly cold, a sure sign that occult forces had also infiltrated this haven of sheer evil.

Chapter Eighteen

Mayo crouched low, his back against a twisted oak tree. .38 in one hand, he clutched a handkerchief in the other, tried to stifle his coughing. He wiped his streaking eyes. Damn it, if only he could see further than a few yards through the drifting smoke.

The distant crackling of the flames was constant, interspersed with loud 'whooshes' as the blaze moved on to more undergrowth.

Then came another sound, much nearer and heavier. Something or somebody was heading his way no more than twenty yards from him. He raised his handgun, steadied it on his other arm. Another wipe of his eyes, a cough which he was unable to stifle. Man or beast?

A brief gap in the swirling smoke allowed a shaft of moonlight to penetrate overhead branches, revealing a huge, dark, hairy shape almost invisible against its dark background.

Shit, it was that wild boar again!

John Mayo's finger rested on the trigger. If the animal advanced further, then a close-range shot was all that could save him. It would also alert Zinovsky and his colleague to his presence. A confrontation in these conditions was a tossup on who would live and who would die.

The wild boar halted, pawed the ground. Its deep-sunk eyes were regarding him, doubtless recalling its most recent kill. It had already fed greedily; its stomach was full. Hunger would not determine its next move.

Still watching him, his scent reminding it of its last narrow escape, that bullet screaming within inches of its body. Death was but a few yards away.

Suddenly the beast turned with amazing rapidity for its bulk. Hooves kicked up the soft woodland soil and within seconds it had vanished into the smoky blackness.

Mayo listened with no small amount of relief to its flight until it was heard no longer. It had tracked him, found him, and then realised that he was as capable of inflicting death on itself.

Right now he had nothing to fear from it, his only threat came from the pair whom he was attempting to track.

An eerie silence followed, just the crackling of the distant raging inferno. Damn it, he could not stand these stifling conditions much longer. He considered returning to the hillside beyond the cottage, maybe seeking refuge down by the winding river below. The thought of immersing his overheated body in fast flowing cold water was tempting.

But no, he had to bring this final encounter with the Devil's henchman and his sidekick to a conclusion. He might not have another opportunity.

He baulked at the prospect of heading towards the fire. Yet…

Suddenly his momentary indecision was interrupted by two shots, the reports close together. They were maybe a hundred yards away, deep in the suffocating darkness.

Certainly they came from those he pursued. His intensive knowledge of firearms told him that the reports came from a .45 handgun. Of course the shots would have been aimed at that devilish hairy monster. It had tracked and found the other two. Was it dead or was it now goring their corpses?

There was only one way to find out and that was to risk the perils of this virtual hell on earth.

Now Zinovsky could see the raging flames, fifty feet high as they roared down the western boundary of the wood, heading towards the road below. Doubtless his own parked car would be reduced to a molten mass but right now that was a minor consideration. Vehicles were easily obtained, their owners slaughtered.

Their only route to safety was to turn about and head eastward. Up there was open moorland, an easy escape route.

He paused momentarily and that was when he felt a tap on the shoulder. His companion, that silent specialist in gruesome torture and executions, sweating inside his heavy clothing, pointed behind them.

'What…' Zinovsky grunted, saw where the other indicated a clearing some distance behind where a brief shaft of moonlight revealed a huge hairy creature.

The wild boar had tracked and located them!

'It is our ally,' his tone lacked confidence. 'Sent by the Master to hunt down Mayo and the girl for us.'

Right now, though, the boar's interest was only in the pair of humans. There was no mistaking its threatening stance, head lowered and poised to charge.

'Something is wrong,' Zinovsky drew his heavy handgun, flicked the safety catch on to 'fire'.

The two shots were in rapid succession, might well have been a single detonation. The boar shuddered in its charge, half reared up and then collapsed in a heap, its legs kicking feebly until finally it lay still on its back. The shots had found their mark.

'It should have been tracking Mayo, not us. Master why are you hunting your loyal servants?' Zinovsky was both puzzled and disturbed.

A terrible fear gripped Zinovsky, and that was when he saw that the inferno had circled the top of the wood and was blazing on the moorland above them. *His planned route of retreat was gone!*

Suddenly, unbelievably, they were trapped within advancing, all blazing undergrowth and trees. *Master, spare us, we have served you well even if we have not located the fugitives who prevented that massacre at the cathedral in the holy city!*

Zinovsky's silent plea went unanswered. Fail the Dark One and there was a terrible price to pay.

'Flee for your life!' An order to the man in black.

The other was bent double, coughing and spewing inside the headgear which covered his features. He made to follow his fleeing master, pitched headlong, clawed frantically for a hold on broken branches but they snapped. His booted feet scrabbled. He half rose, fell back.

'Help me!' A throaty plea but Zinovsky was only concerned for his own safety. He realised that the one he served had ignored his pleading. He had shot Satan's monster, the penalty was death, burned by this terrible inferno which had surely been sent from the bowels of hell.

Mayo saw and shuddered in spite of the increasing heat. One final glimpse of his deadly foe, arms raised in a final plea to the one he served. His screams were drowned in the fiery crackling and then he fell and was lost to sight, gone forever in a bizarre unholy cremation.

John Mayo's only thought now was for his own safety. He turned about, found a track which appeared to be heading downhill, followed it. Twice he had to deviate where falling branches barred his progress. The smoke was less thick here, his vision improved.

Then, much to his relief, he emerged above the cottage. Beyond the neighbouring farm the firefighters had checked the advancing wall of flames. It headed down towards the road and would probably burn itself out when it reached the river.

He grimaced as he passed the bloody remains of the man who had once been Richardson. Foxes and corvids would probably clear it up. More importantly Zinovsky was dead, his UK followers would now be without a leader as would their European counterparts.

That only left Hamza bin Laden in hiding somewhere abroad with a huge reward offered for his capture. Some of the Al-Qaeda jihadists might be tempted. Only time would tell.

Back in the cottage Mayo made a couple of phone calls. The first was to the Jones family to reassure them that their home was safe. The second was to Charlie Wells advising him of

Zinovsky's demise and suggesting that an armed unit raid that home in Lichfield.

That done, Mayo sank back into an armchair. Right now he would take a well-earned rest.

Another mission had been completed. He promised himself that this one was his last, a vow he had made on more than one occasion in the past.

Tomorrow he would head north, re-join Gwenda and pick up the traces of their leisurely retirement. He attempted to convince himself that there would be no more missions. This one would be his very last.

He pursed his lips and a sense of doubt crept into his vow. He had made such promises to himself in the past and they had proved to be futile.

He let out a deep sigh as he packed his few belongings into a holdall. Right now he preferred not to even think about what the future might hold. Whatever would be, would be.

ABOUT THE AUTHOR

Guy N. Smith has been a best-selling author for over 40 years. He has written over 70 horror novels since 1975 as well as numerous short stories in the genre.

Find out more at www.guynsmith.com

Also from the Sinister Horror Company

The Charnel Caves: A Crabs Novel

Horror lurked in the maze of cliff caves where a new generation of giant crabs were breeding.

In 1975 an army of gigantic crabs, the result of an underwater nuclear experiment, attacked the Welsh coastline.

The battle was bloody, many lives were lost until the crustacean invaders were defeated.

Over the ensuing years they turned up in the oceans of the World with further terrible slaughter of humans. Finally, though, it was believed that these monsters from the deep had been eradicated. Only memories of their invasions of land remained with the older inhabitants, tales of their depredations on mankind were whispered but often ridiculed by the modern generations.

Until a few of the survivors returned to the Welsh coast and began breeding secretly in a maze of caverns beneath the cliffs, preparing for a further attack on mankind.

Guy N. Smith Illustrated Bibliography

"The sheer effort and dedication that's gone into creating this unbelievably comprehensive bibliography is breath-taking." – DLS Reviews

The complete(ish) guide to collecting the works of Guy N. Smith.

A journey into collecting the works of prolific author Guy Newman Smith. The book covers all genres of the Great Scribbler's writing and contains over 950 pictures and useful details to assist any would-be collector.

Guy N. Smith Illustrated Bibliography

The author has endeavoured to list and visually represent, through over 950 colour pictures, the vast catalogue of output from Guy N. Smith's 65+ years in print; from the early stories he had published in the Tettenhall Observer and Advertiser paper as a teenager through to the present day. A career that crosses fiction and non-fiction and has covered almost all possible genres along the way, from Self-Sufficiency to Westerns, via Countryside and Glamour magazines of the 70s, all in addition to the numerous horror and thriller titles he is better known for.

Content includes Fiction (all imprints/editions inc. non UK) and Non-Fiction Categories: Horror, Thriller, Countryside and Children's Novels, Omnibus Collections, Chapbooks, Graphic Novels, Anthologies, Fanzines, Booklets, Magazines (70s adult Glamour, Country Sport, Game-keeping, Horror etc.), Periodicals and Newspapers.

The book also contains an original Guy N. Smith short story 'The Beast in the Cage' along with humorous insight into the levels of collecting Guy N. Smith's works in 'The Completist- A Cautionary Tale' by author Shane P.D Agnew.

The Sinister Horror Company is an independent UK publisher of genre fiction. Their mission a simple one – to write, publish and launch innovative and exciting genre fiction.

For further information on the Sinister Horror Company visit:

SinisterHorrorCompany.com
Facebook.com/sinisterhorrorcompany
Twitter @SinisterHC

SINISTERHORRORCOMPANY.COM

www.ingramcontent.com/pod-product-compliance
Ingram Content Group UK Ltd.
Pitfield, Milton Keynes, MK11 3LW, UK
UKHW020223250726
13967UKWH00001B/155

9 781912 578313